*The Little Silver House*

*Also by Jennie D. Lindquist*

THE GOLDEN NAME DAY

# The Little Silver House

## by
### JENNIE D. LINDQUIST
Author of THE GOLDEN NAME DAY

### Pictures by
### GARTH WILLIAMS

HARPER & ROW, PUBLISHERS

New York and Evanston

**THE LITTLE SILVER HOUSE**

*Text copyright* © *1959 by Jennie Dorothea Lindquist*

*Pictures copyright* © *1959 by Garth Williams*

All rights reserved. Printed in the United States of America. No part of this book may be used or reproduced in any manner whatsoever without written permission except in the case of brief quotations embodied in critical articles and reviews. For information address Harper & Row, Publishers, Inc., 10 East 53rd Street, New York, N.Y. 10022.

*Library of Congress catalog card number: 59-8975*

*The Little Silver House*

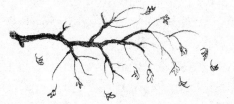

## Chapter 1

THE year Nancy was staying with Grandma and Grandpa Benson, the children had an unexpected vacation in the fall. There was a fire in the town school, and it had to be closed two weeks for repairs.

The vacation turned out to be an unusual one. For a long time afterward, Nancy and the Carlson girls spoke of it as "the topsy-turvy weeks."

When Grandpa came home to supper on Saturday, the day after the fire, he did not even wait to feed his horse, Karl the Twelfth, before he came into the house. Instead he hurried into the kitchen with a telegram in his hand. Grandma turned pale. She thought a telegram meant bad news. But Grandpa called out:

"*Good* news! George and Hanna are coming!"

"George and Hanna!" said Grandma, so surprised that she sat right down in her rocking chair.

She and Grandpa usually spoke English when Nancy was with them, but now, in their excitement, they began to talk Swedish.

"My goodness!" Grandma said at last. "Here we sit talking and Nancy doesn't know what it's all about. You must forgive us, darling. This is the best news we've had for a long time. Come, I'll tell you about it while we put supper on the table and Grandpa feeds Karl the Twelfth."

Nancy had often heard about Aunt Hanna and Uncle George. Hanna and Grandma had been playmates in Sweden and, as young girls, they had come to America together. George and Grandpa had been great friends since they were boys. After they were married they had lived next door to each other while their children were growing up. Now Uncle George and Aunt Hanna lived far away in Chicago, but they were still Grandma's and Grandpa's best friends.

"It is more than ten years since we have seen them," said Grandma.

"*Ten years!*" said Nancy. "That's more years than I have lived."

"Yes," said Grandma. "Sigrid was a tiny baby when they were here last. You remember I told you last week that they had come East because their son was sick. When I saw the telegram, I was afraid he was worse, but he is much better; so they can come to see us, too, before they go back home."

"When will they come?" asked Nancy.

"Tomorrow afternoon at five and stay until Wednesday. I can't believe it yet. We must have the Carlsons here for supper tomorrow night, and Uncle Sven and Aunt Martha, too. They'll all be so happy."

"Can we decorate the house for the company?" asked Nancy.

"Of course," said Grandma. "Aunt Hanna loves flowers. You and the other girls can decorate tomorrow afternoon."

"We can get wild purple asters and goldenrod," said Nancy.

"Yes," said Grandma, "and there are a few flowers left in the garden."

Nancy could see that the telegram had made

Grandma and Grandpa very happy indeed. They spent all evening aking plans and getting ready for their visitor

"It feels like Christmas," Nancy said early Sunday afternoon when Uncle John and Aunt Anna Carlson, and Sigrid, Elsa, and Helga came. When Uncle Sven and Aunt Martha drove into the yard, the children ran out to meet them and to give their horse, Whoa Emma, some sugar.

"Nancy says it feels like Christmas," said Elsa, "and it does."

"I once read a story," said Aunt Martha, "in which there was a woman everybody loved. The story said that when she came into a room it was as if candles had been lighted. That always made me think of Aunt Hanna; and it's like Uncle George, too. It *is* like Christmas when they come."

They all went into the kitchen.

"Grandma says we can pick some goldenrod and asters to decorate the house," said Nancy.

"I'll come with you," said Grandpa. "Then we can get some autumn leaves, too. This is *storfrämmande* we're having today."

"What's that?" asked Nancy.

"I know," said Elsa. "*Storfrämmande* means very, very important company."

"Like kings and queens," said Sigrid.

"That's the idea," said Grandpa.

"Yes, that's right," said Grandma, smiling at the children. "True friends like Aunt Hanna and Uncle George are as important as kings and queens, so you must make the house look especially pretty."

"Grandma," said Nancy, "if they're as important as kings and queens, could we make flower crowns for them?"

"That would be nice," said Grandma.

"I have never seen a child who loves flowers as much as you do, Nancy," said Aunt Anna. "You remind me of your mother. Your father used to say she could pick up a wilted flower in the street and take it home and make a lovely plant of it. And you are going to be just like her."

Nancy smiled. She loved to be told that she was like her mother.

"But I never knew about flower crowns until I came here and Grandma showed me," she said, "and I love to make them."

"So do I," said Aunt Martha, "and I'll help you when you get back. There isn't much time."

"No, the afternoon's going fast," said Grandpa. "Come along, girls."

"I'll go, too," said Uncle Sven, "unless I'm needed here."

"One man is all we need," said Aunt Anna, "and John will help us." So the flower-gathering party set out.

Not far from Grandpa's house there was a little wood and near it a field where goldenrod and wild purple asters were in blossom.

"Purple and gold are the right colors for kings and queens," said Sigrid, and the children began to pick the flowers while Grandpa and Uncle Sven went to gather branches. When they came back with their lovely colored leaves, each little girl had her arms full of the purple and golden flowers.

"It's getting very hot and sultry for late September," said Uncle Sven. "It feels as if there might be a thundershower."

"Oh, dear!" said Helga. "What if it rains on the *storfrämmande!*"

"It does feel like a thundershower," said Grandpa, "but rain won't hurt anybody, not even *storfrämmande*, Helga, so we won't worry."

They were all glad, though, to get back to the cool house where Grandma had milk ready for the children and coffee for the grownups so they could rest a little before they began to decorate.

Aunt Martha had been up in the attic and found some thin wire which she had formed into the shape of crowns. They did not usually use wire when they made crowns—just leaves and flowers.

"But we have so little time today," she said, "that I thought it would be better if we had wire frames to start on."

She had been out in the garden, and had brought in some of Grandma's large purple asters and tiny golden marigolds.

"The marigolds are better for crowns than goldenrod," she said.

They decided to make Uncle George's crown from red and gold autumn leaves with one big purple aster at the front.

"That is an amethyst," said Sigrid.

"The Royal Amethyst," said Elsa, "that no one but the King is ever allowed to wear."

They made Aunt Hanna's crown of green leaves, marigolds, and small wild asters.

"Emeralds and amethysts and flowers made of gold," said Elsa.

Meanwhile, the grownups were filling crocks and jars with goldenrod and asters and putting autumn branches over windows and doors.

"Like Christmas greens," said Nancy, "only different colors. It's beautiful."

"It will make Aunt Hanna so happy," said Grandma. "She will remember how we used to decorate our homes when we were children in Sweden. We didn't have many pretty things in those days, but we did have leaves and flowers. I'd rather have them than real amethysts and emeralds," she added, smiling at the children.

When it was time for Grandpa and Karl the Twelfth to go to the station, the children went upstairs to put on their Sunday-best white dresses. Nancy's and Elsa's had blue sashes; Sigrid's and Helga's sashes were pink.

Now everything was ready. The children ran downstairs to admire the house and the royal crowns once more.

"I hope they'll talk about the olden time tonight," said Elsa. "I love to hear about how it was then."

"They will," said Sigrid. "Grownups always do when they haven't seen each other for a long time."

"It's getting hotter and hotter," said Aunt Martha. "There's thunder in the air all right."

"We need rain," said Uncle Sven, "but now that it has waited so long, I hope it holds off until the travelers get here."

"There goes Oscar!" said Nancy, and they all hurried to the door. Oscar could always hear Karl the Twelfth coming before anyone else did.

In a minute he was back, running along beside the wagon, and barking a welcome. Karl the Twelfth drew up beside the door—and then, what excitement! What talking and laughing and hugging and kissing!

When Aunt Hanna and Uncle George stepped into the house and saw the autumn leaves and flowers, their cries of surprise and pleasure delighted the children. Aunt Hanna even had tears in her eyes, she was so happy.

"Oh, Albertina," she said to Grandma, "how it takes me back to the time when we were children."

"I knew it would," said Grandma. "I told the girls so. And they have a surprise for you that will take you back even more. But you will want to go to your room now and we'll have supper on the table when you come down again."

"They're going to talk about the olden time," sang Helga after the company had gone upstairs. "They're going to talk about the olden time."

"And that will suit you fine, won't it, young lady?" said Uncle John, picking her up and swinging her onto his shoulder.

"Uncle John," said Nancy, "hold her like that and let her crown the King and Queen."

"Because she's the youngest," said Sigrid.

9

"I'll get the crowns," said Elsa.

The visitors soon came downstairs. Aunt Hanna had put on a dress of soft lavender silk. Helga carefully set the flower crown on her head.

"You look *beautiful*," said Elsa.

"Lavender is exactly the right color to go with a crown of purple and gold," said Sigrid.

"Don't I look beautiful, too?" asked Uncle George, making such a low bow, after Helga had crowned him, that his crown fell over one ear.

"No," said Helga, "you look funny. But," she added quickly, "you look as if you must be awfully nice."

That made everybody laugh. But, then, they were all so happy around the big dining room table that night that practically everything made them laugh.

Nobody even noticed that the weather was growing more and more sultry, until suddenly there was a loud noise of thunder. The wind began to blow and the rain came down in torrents. Everybody hurried to shut the windows upstairs and down.

"It's good to have the rain at last," said Uncle Sven when they were all back at the table again.

They were still sitting there, talking and laughing, when the clock struck eight.

"One more thing I must ask before we get up," said Uncle George. "Is the boarded-up house still standing?"

"*A boarded-up* house!" said Elsa, forgetting that children must not interrupt grownups.

The minute she had spoken she grew pink with embarrassment, but Uncle George turned to answer her.

"Yes," he said. "It belonged to a family that owned a great deal of property in town. Crane, their name was. They moved away, but before they went they sold all their property except this one little house in the country. I suppose they expected to use it as a summer cottage to come back to; but that must have been thirty years ago."

"Boarded up for thirty years!" Sigrid said. "I wonder *why!*"

"Children!" said Aunt Anna. "Where are your manners? Uncle George asked a question and you don't give anyone a chance to answer it."

But neither she nor any of the other grownups could help smiling at the girls' eagerness.

"As far as I know, it's still standing," said Uncle Sven, "but I haven't been out that way for a long time."

"We haven't either," said Grandpa, "though

it's not very far and that pine woods near the house is a good place to picnic in."

"We had so many happy times there long ago," said Grandma, "but it never seemed the same after you and Hanna left, George. I guess that's why we got out of the habit of going there. I remember you always liked that little house."

"Yes, I did," said Uncle George. "And not only the house, but the way it stands there in the valley with the woods behind it and the hills back of that. It's a funny thing—none of us was ever in that house; yet often out in Chicago I think of it, and of what a good place it would be to settle down in."

"I wonder what happened to the Crane family," said Aunt Hanna. "Do any of them ever come back here?"

"I don't know," said Aunt Martha, "but I did drive by the house once last year and it was still boarded up then. The Cranes must have made some arrangements to have it cared for, because the roof is well mended and none of the boards is loose. I don't know why we don't drive out that road more often. It's a lovely road, although it's pretty well overgrown with grass now."

"I'd like to see that little place again," said Uncle George.

"I'll take some time off tomorrow," said Grandpa, "and we'll drive out that way."

"Why not go tonight?" said Uncle George.

"*Tonight!*" said Grandma.

"In all this rain?" asked Aunt Hanna.

"It stopped raining a few minutes ago," said Uncle George. "Look out of the window; the moon is shining."

And so it was. They had been so busy talking and laughing that they had not even noticed that the rain had stopped.

"Why don't you men go?" asked Aunt Hanna. "We ladies will stay at home and do the dishes and visit."

"Nonsense!" said Uncle George. "Four men can't go on a moonlight ride alone. We'll take these four beautiful young ladies who are all dressed up in their best dresses. What do you say, Erik? Karl the Twelfth can carry them and one man to drive, can't he? We can take turns riding and walking. It's not more than three miles, I'm sure."

"But it's already after eight," said Aunt Anna, "and it will be close to ten before you get back."

"Oh, Mamma, please let us go," said Elsa. "*Please.* We never went on a moonlight ride."

Aunt Anna began to laugh.

"George, you haven't changed a bit," she said. "Who but you would ever take such a notion? Get your coats, girls, but don't get out of the wagon. You haven't got your rubbers here and the grass will be wet."

"Grandpa," said Nancy, "could Alex come, too? All the Crimson Ramblers ought to go."

"Well, I don't know what his mother will think," said Grandpa doubtfully, but, like Nancy, he hated to see Alex left out of anything. "If you'll harness Karl the Twelfth, John," he added, "I'll go speak to Mrs. Brown."

"Who are the Crimson Ramblers?" asked Uncle George.

"Oh, it's a club we've got," said Sigrid. "All of us belong, and Alex does, and Grandpa and Karl the Twelfth and Oscar."

"And Grandpa and Karl the Twelfth usually take us for a ride on Sunday," said Nancy, "and so I thought Alex ought to come, too."

"And who is Alex?" asked Uncle George.

"He's a boy that lives across the street," said Nancy.

"He can't walk," said Helga. "He can only go around in his wheel chair."

"But he's the most fun of any boy I know," said Elsa.

*15*

"Well, that sounds to me like a pretty good club," said Uncle George.

Grandpa came back in a few minutes carrying a happy Alex in his arms. Karl the Twelfth was ready. Nancy, Helga, and Elsa got into the back seat. Sigrid, Alex, and Grandpa sat in front. The other three men took the first turn at walking, and Oscar trotted along beside them.

"Grandpa," Elsa asked, "why didn't you ever tell us about the boarded-up house?"

"I never realized that you'd be so much interested," said Grandpa, "and now I'm afraid you'll be disappointed. I think you're picturing it as something mysterious and exciting, and it's just a plain little house."

"But it's what's inside that matters," said Alex. "There might be treasure buried in the cellar."

"There might be treasure under your kitchen sink," Uncle Sven teased him, "or hidden under the roof in Danny's doghouse at the farm, but I don't think there is. Still, I agree that any house in which people have lived is interesting."

"Somebody must have loved it or they wouldn't want to keep it all these years," said Elsa.

"I think you're right, Elsa," said Uncle George, "although I know that some people refuse to sell a house just because they're stubborn and don't want anybody else to get it. Wait until you see it, children, and then you can tell us what you think of it. Meanwhile, isn't it lovely in the moonlight? Could we sing, John, do you think, or would we disturb people?"

"Not so early as this if we sing softly," said Uncle John, who could never resist any opportunity to sing.

So very softly the four men sang some of the lovely old Swedish songs the Carlson girls had heard ever since they were babies—songs that Nancy, too, had grown to love since she had come to stay with the Bensons.

"It's getting dark," said Helga. "Is it going to rain again?"

"Oh, no," said Uncle John, "it's just the moon going behind the clouds. It will come out again."

And that's how it was the rest of the way: sometimes the moon shone brightly; sometimes it hid its face.

"It's more interesting than plain moonlight," said Elsa.

After a time Grandpa got out to walk and Uncle Sven took his turn at driving. At last they came to the road of the little house. It was very dark now, for the moon seemed to have gone behind the clouds for good. Grandpa unfastened the lantern from the back of the wagon and walked in front of Karl the Twelfth, leading him over the uneven road.

"I'm almost scared," said Helga, shivering.

"Me, too," said Nancy happily.

"We're nearly there," said Grandpa. "I'm afraid we're not going to see much."

But at that moment the moon came out and shone in all its brightness on the little house. There it stood with its weather-beaten gray boards, still wet from the rain, glistening in the moonlight.

"Why, it's *silver!*" said Helga.

"It is!" said Elsa. "A little silver house!"

"You never told us," said Nancy, "that it was a little *silver* house."

The grownups smiled. There was no doubt about it—although by morning the little house would be plain gray again, tonight it was made of silver. They stood silently, looking at it.

"I think the moon is trying to show it to us," said Sigrid. "The house is so bright and the woods back of it and the hills are so dark. How many rooms does it have, do you think?"

"Oh, probably five," said Uncle George, "a sitting room and a dining room and a kitchen downstairs, and two small bedrooms up under the roof."

"It's the most beautiful house I ever saw in all my life," said Nancy.

Uncle George began to sing again and the other three men joined him. Neither Nancy nor Alex knew the song, but Nancy thought the lovely melody seemed to fit the little house. Later, Grandpa told her what the words meant. "Something like this," he said.

"I know a house, a little house among the mountains,
  A little house I call my own.
  It matters not how far away I travel,
  That little house is in my heart forever.
  It waits there in its green and pleasant valley—
  The little house I love to call my own."

The song ended but the moon went on shining, and it was hard to leave when Grandpa turned Karl the Twelfth around and they started for home.

It was too late now to sing along the roadway, and none of the children talked much. Helga fell asleep, sitting between Nancy and Elsa.

"Let's go back soon," Elsa whispered.

"Yes," said Nancy. But that was all. Tonight it was enough just to have seen the little house, all silver in the moonlight.

*19*

*Chapter 2*

THE next morning when Nancy came down to breakfast she found Grandma and Aunt Hanna in the kitchen. Grandpa and Uncle George had already gone to Grandpa's store. Teddy, the cat, sat by the stove.

He was known throughout the neighborhood as "the cat that drinks coffee." Every morning when Grandpa had his breakfast he gave Teddy a saucer of coffee with plenty of cream and sugar. The morning after Nancy came to the Bensons', Teddy discovered that she could easily be persuaded to give him a second helping and he was on hand every day to remind her. Now Aunt Hanna had to see this famous cat drinking his coffee. She laughed and patted him.

"Your name may be Theodore Roosevelt," she said, "but you are a real Swedish cat anyway."

Teddy jumped into her lap and settled down for an after-coffee nap. So there they sat in Grandma's pleasant kitchen—Grandma, Aunt Hanna, Nancy, and Teddy—with the geraniums blossoming in the windows and the sun shining on the blue-and-white checked tablecloth.

"Eat your oatmeal," said Grandma to Nancy, "before you tell us about the little house."

While she was eating, Grandma told Aunt Hanna about Nancy's school.

"You know that when Nancy came to us in April she wasn't very well, and the doctor said she must stay outdoors and rest a great deal. Now you can see how well she looks, but, of course, she got behind with her schoolwork; so Mrs. Brown suggested that this fall she have her lessons with Alex. She used to be a teacher and she will see to it that Nancy makes up the work she lost so that when she goes back home, she can go right into her own class just as if she had never been away at all."

"Isn't that nice!" said Aunt Hanna. "For

Nancy and Alex, too. Do you like this kind of school, dear?"

"Oh, yes," said Nancy. "It's fun. Mrs. Brown reads to us and tells us stories and everything."

"But they have to study hard, too," said Grandma. "She is a good teacher and a wonderful mother, and she has had a hard time. Alex's father died when Alex was a baby. He will never be able to walk, but he is such a smart boy. We all think the world of him, don't we, Nancy?"

"Yes, we do," said Nancy. "And Grandpa says he'll make his mark in the world even if he can't walk."

But now she couldn't wait another minute to talk about the little house.

"Alex thought there might be treasure hidden in the little house," she said, "and that that was why it was boarded up. I don't know about that but you should have seen it! It was *silver*, a little silver house!"

Aunt Hanna smiled at her. "I can imagine how it looked," she said. "I'd like to see that little house again myself."

"Maybe Grandpa will drive us out that way sometime tomorrow," said Grandma. "This afternoon we're going down to Aunt Anna's, Nancy. She's having a coffee party so that some of the

ladies who knew Aunt Hanna when she lived here will have a chance to see her again."

Nancy finished her breakfast; they talked a little longer about the silver house, and then she went upstairs to make her bed.

Aunt Hanna went with her to see the yellow rose wallpaper Grandma had let her choose when she first came.

"Yellow roses are my favorite flower," Nancy said.

Aunt Hanna stopped to see Nancy's doll, Charlotte, too, and all her pretty clothes. She looked at Nancy's tiny doll, only about four inches high, and all the dresses Nancy had made for her.

It was easy to make a dress for this doll. All you had to do was cut a circle out of cloth, make a hole in the middle to slip over the doll's head, make two more holes for her arms to go through, and tie a sash around her waist.

"The Carlson girls all have dolls like this," said Nancy, "and so does Wanda, a girl that lives across the road from Aunt Martha's farm. We play with them more than we do with our big dolls. These are all named for flowers. This is Jasmine; Sigrid's doll is Marigold; Helga's is Daisy; and Wanda's is Violet.

"But Elsa chose a funny flower name for hers. Hers is Trillium!"

Aunt Hanna laughed.

"I think Elsa must be the kind of little girl who never does anything quite the way anyone else does," she said.

"That's just the kind of girl she is," said Nancy. "I love to play with her. All the girls and Alex are fun to play with, but Elsa is more fun than anybody else in the world."

"You're having a good time at Grandma Benson's, aren't you?" asked Aunt Hanna.

"Oh, yes," said Nancy, "and I didn't even want to come at first. When Mamma had to go to the hospital, and Papa said I was going to stay with the Bensons, I cried. They aren't really my grandmother and grandfather, you know. They're friends of Mamma's. I guess I didn't know how nice they'd be to me. Anyway, I cried when Papa told me."

"Of course you did," said Aunt Hanna. "It must have been hard to go away all by yourself."

"I love it here now, though," said Nancy. "I love the country and all the animals. In the city I couldn't have any pets. And I love all the Swedish things we do, too. Before I came here, I didn't even know about things like name days and making flower crowns, and everything. Grandpa says I'm getting to be a real little Swedish girl."

"And Grandma tells me your mother is getting better," said Aunt Hanna.

"Yes, she is," said Nancy. "She can write me quite a lot of letters now."

"Nancy! Time for school!" Grandma called, and Nancy ran across the street to Alex's house.

While she and Alex were sitting on the piazza having a midmorning glass of milk, the Carlson girls came up the street.

"Hi!" Sigrid called. "Mamma said we could come to see you just while you're having recess."

"I wish you were having vacation, too," said Elsa.

"So do I," said Alex. "We asked Mamma if we could, but she said no."

"She said we could do something special some day, though," said Nancy, "and invite you to visit."

"Oh, that's good," said Sigrid. "I'd love to visit school."

"What I'd like to do," said Nancy, "is go and see that little house again. Wasn't it beautiful?"

"It's the first time I ever saw a little silver house," said Elsa. "I didn't know houses could be silver."

"Well, of course it isn't really," said Alex. "I don't suppose it looks beautiful at all in the daytime. It's just an ordinary old gray house."

"It is not!" said Nancy and Elsa together.

"That house just couldn't be ordinary," said Elsa. "There must be something very special about it."

"And it *is* beautiful," said Nancy.

"Well, anyway," said Sigrid, "it seems as if there must be something strange about it. Boarded up for thirty years! I can't imagine why."

"I was hoping there might be treasure in it," said Alex, "but after I saw it I didn't think there would be. I know what it would be good for, though. It would be good for us to have for a Crimson Rambler Clubhouse."

"A clubhouse all our own, you mean?" asked Helga.

"Yes," said Alex.

"Well, we can't have it, that's one sure thing," said Sigrid, "but it would be fun. We could make curtains for the windows."

"And paper the walls," said Elsa.

"Yellow rose wallpaper in one bedroom," said Nancy.

"And blue forget-me-not paper in the other," said Sigrid.

"No, ships or horses or something like that," said Alex.

"And a garden," said Nancy.

"And a little stove, and we could cook?" asked Helga.

"But where would we get the money?" asked Sigrid.

"I don't know," said Nancy. "I guess we couldn't, but I wish we could find out something about the little house. I'd like to know who used to live there, and if they had any children. I can't think why they'd leave it. A little silver house!"

Mrs. Brown's telephone rang. They heard her going to answer it, and in a few minutes she came out on the piazza looking troubled.

"Alex," she said, "Grandmother Brown has broken her arm and we must get ready at once to go to her. We'll come back as soon as we can, but I'm afraid, Nancy, you'll have a vacation after all. Will you run across and explain to Grandma, please?"

Nancy and Elsa both ran across the street. They came back almost immediately. Grandma was with them; she had come to see if there was anything she could do to help Mrs. Brown get ready.

"I never saw such mixed-up days," said Nancy. "I wonder what's going to happen next."

"Goodness, I don't know," said Alex. "I'm sorry Grandmother broke her arm, but I wish we didn't have to go away now. There's too much going on. If you find out anything more about the little house, be sure to write and tell me."

"We will," said Elsa, "and if anything else exciting happens, we'll tell you that, too."

The girls had a lovely afternoon. They sat in the Carlsons' back yard making dresses for their little dolls and talking about the silver house. The ladies at Aunt Hanna's party seemed to be having a good time, too; they were talking and laughing. But Aunt Hanna, even at her own party, did not forget the children. She excused herself long enough to come out to show them how to make flower hats for their dolls.

"Take a ribbon like this," she said, "or a strip of cloth, and run a thread with tiny stitches along one edge of it. It is better to have your thread double so it will be stronger. When you get to the end of the ribbon, pull the thread, and the ribbon will be gathered, and you can shape it into a little hat. Like this. Then fasten your thread

firmly and sew the two ends of the ribbon together."

Sure enough! There was a little hat. It looked
like a pink flower.

"If you use cloth," said Aunt Hanna, "you
can scallop the outside edge to look like petals.
Or you can use two pieces of cloth or ribbon,
one a little wider than the other, and you will
have a double flower. Take a piece of coarse yellow embroidery thread and sew over and over
in the middle so that the flower will have a yellow
center."

The girls were delighted.

"We should each make a hat to match our
child's name," said Sigrid. "I'm going to try to
find some orange-colored cloth or bright yellow
to make a marigold hat."

"Will you help me make a daisy, Sigrid?"
asked Helga.

"Yes, I will," said Sigrid, "and we'll tell Wanda
and she can make a violet. But I don't know how
Nancy's and Elsa's flowers look."

"I don't either," said Nancy. "I chose Jasmine
because I've read about jasmine flowers and I
love the name."

"We'll ask Miss Bates at the library," said Elsa.
"She'll help us find a picture and I'll look at

trillium again. It has only three big petals and I think the center is red. It will be a different-looking hat. People will say, 'What an unusual hat!' And I'll say, 'It's the latest style from Paris!' "

Aunt Hanna laughed. "Good for you!" she said. "I don't believe I ever saw any jasmine either, Nancy, but I think I've read of yellow jasmine, though perhaps it comes in other colors, too. And I think it has a very sweet smell."

"I hope it's yellow," said Nancy; "it's my favorite color."

"Mamma will let us have a little of her perfumery," said Helga, "to make our hats smell sweet."

"And when I get home," said Aunt Hanna, "I'll send you some pieces of cloth and ribbon of different colors, so that you can make more than one kind of hat each."

"And we can make dresses to match," said Sigrid. "Aunt Hanna, you are so good to us."

Aunt Hanna went back into the house, but in a few minutes Uncle George walked into the yard.

"Grandpa has to stay in the store for a while," he said, "but I've come to have a visit with you girls. Ladies' coffee parties are all very well for ladies, but I thought we could take a walk downtown and have our party in the ice-cream parlor. How do you like that idea?"

There was no doubt that the girls liked it very much indeed. They did not often have a chance to go to the ice-cream parlor.

"We'll ask Mamma," said Sigrid.

"She has already said you may go," said Uncle George.

All the way downtown they talked about the little house.

"I can see that you like it as well as I do," said Uncle George.

"I wish it was nearer to us, though," said Sigrid, "so we could walk out to it now and then."

"If only it was out Aunt Martha's way instead of in the opposite direction, we could see it often," said Nancy.

"Anyway, I'm so glad you remembered it, Uncle George," said Elsa. "If you hadn't come, we might never even have heard of it. But I wish we could find out more about it."

"I tell you what," said Uncle George, "if old Mr. Maple is in his ice-cream parlor, we'll ask him. I remember he was a great one for knowing all about what went on in town."

When they got to the ice-cream parlor they found Mr. Maple's son at the counter.

"Pa just stepped out for a few minutes," he said, in answer to Uncle George's question. "He'll be right back. Can I serve you some ice cream while you're waiting?"

"Not plain ice cream for us today," said Uncle George. "College ices all round, please."

"College ices!" said Sigrid. "My goodness, we've hardly ever had those. They cost so much. I think they're ten cents each," she added in a worried tone.

"And well worth it for an occasion like this," said Uncle George. "What kind have you?"

"Maple walnut, chocolate walnut, strawberry, and pineapple. And a new kind we're trying out—cherry."

"Make your choice, girls," said Uncle George. This took time and thought, but at last they decided. Sigrid and Uncle George chose maple walnut; Helga decided on chocolate walnut. Nancy and Elsa tried the new kind—vanilla ice cream with bright red candied cherries.

"Poor ladies at home, having only coffee and things," said Elsa.

They sat at one of the round marble-topped tables and slowly ate their treat.

"I hope Mr. Maple comes back," said Elsa, "but I'm glad he isn't here yet. One thing at a time is enough when it's as good as a college ice."

They were almost through when he came in. He was delighted to see Uncle George and wanted to hear all about him and his family. Then Uncle George wanted to hear all about Mr. Maple's family, so it was quite a while before they got to the little silver house.

But at last Uncle George said, "We were speaking last night about the Crane family and the little house they never wanted to sell."

"The one out near the Lake Road, that's still boarded up, you mean? Yes, I remember about that. There was a good deal of talk about it when the Cranes left town. They would have liked to get rid of it, all right, but they couldn't."

"Couldn't?" asked Uncle George.

"Weren't allowed to, I mean," said Mr. Maple. "Old Jacob Crane built the house and lived in it for many years. When he died he left a will that said the house couldn't be sold. It had to be kept in the family. It was an ornery thing to do because now nobody gets any good out of the place. Will Crane who owned the big house on the hill here in town tried his best to have the

*35*

will changed but he couldn't do it. Law is law. I didn't care much for him; he thought so highly of himself, he'd hardly speak to us common fellows. But, all the same, I hate to see anybody tied up by something his ancestors decided."

"Couldn't they rent the place?" asked Uncle George.

"No, something about that in the will, too," said Mr. Maple. "Old Jacob left money, I understand, so the house would be well cared for; and it has been."

Uncle George looked at the children.

"These girls," he said, "have taken a great fancy to that little house."

"Is that so?" said Mr. Maple. "Well, it's a pretty little place."

"Maybe," said Elsa shyly, "Old Jacob loved it so much that he couldn't bear to let anybody but his own family have it."

"Maybe," said Mr. Maple doubtfully, "but it seems to me a funny way to love something—tie it up so nobody can use it. Plain ornery, it seems to me."

"How did he arrange to have it cared for?" asked Uncle George.

"Through his lawyer, I expect," said Mr. Maple. "Jim Fitch, a farmer who lived up the road a piece, used to have the care of it, but I don't know who does now."

They sat a little longer talking and then Uncle George and the girls said thank you to Mr. Maple and his son, and went out into the September sunshine.

"I wonder about Old Jacob," said Elsa. "Does ornery mean the same as contrary, Uncle George?"

"Just about the same."

"I thought it did, the way Mr. Maple said it. But maybe Old Jacob really wasn't ornery; maybe he did love the little house."

"I think Mr. Maple was right," said Sigrid. "Old Jacob shouldn't have fixed it so that nobody could use it."

"Maybe he didn't mean to," said Nancy. "Maybe he loved the house so much he was sure some of his family would always want to live in it. I don't see how they could help wanting to."

"Let's go back this way," said Uncle George, turning a corner onto a street that was lined with maple trees, now changing from green to gold and scarlet.

"I love autumn," said Elsa, "the leaves and the feeling of it and the smell in the air."

"I do, too," said Uncle George, "and I don't

believe there is any place in the world where autumn is as beautiful as it is here in New England."

"The woods back of the little house must be lovely now in the daytime," said Elsa.

"When I came in April," said Nancy, "Grandpa said to watch every day and I did. I never saw spring come in the country before and it was wonderful."

"All times of year are wonderful," said Uncle George, "each in its own way. When you came, everything was waking up. Now everything is going to sleep for a while."

"But before they go to bed, the trees are going to have a big party," said Elsa, "and they are getting all dressed up for it. The maples got ready first, I don't know why, but . . ."

"Perhaps they are on the program," said Nancy.

"That's it," said Elsa. "The maples have to be ready early because they are going to do the dance of the autumn leaves. They practice every night after people have gone to bed."

"I wish I could see them," said Helga.

"I wish I could see all the hours of the night and the day," said Elsa. "We get up at seven in the morning and only stay up until eight at night, or once in a while until nine; and there are all those hours in between when we don't see what is happening."

"You know, that gives me an idea," said Uncle George.

"What is it?" asked Nancy. "Are you going to fix it so we can stay up all the hours of the night?"

"No," said Uncle George, laughing. "That I can't do. But maybe we can do something special tomorrow, if you'll all go to bed very early to-night."

"Does it have something to do with the little silver house?" asked Sigrid.

"No, nothing to do with the little house."

"I heard Aunt Martha say this afternoon that she and Uncle Sven want us all to come to the farm while you are here," said Elsa. "Are we going? Does it have something to do with that?"

"Oh, I love to go to the farm," said Helga. "Please tell us what it is, Uncle George."

But Uncle George wouldn't tell, no matter how much they begged.

"Let's stop teasing," said Sigrid at last. "It's really more exciting not to know."

"Yes, I guess it is," said Elsa. "Just think, if there hadn't been a fire in our school, we wouldn't be having a vacation, and tomorrow would be an ordinary day."

"And if Uncle George hadn't come," said Nancy, "we might never have found the little silver house."

"And if Old Jacob hadn't been ornery," said Sigrid, "it wouldn't have been a boarded-up house at all."

"I don't believe he was ornery," said Elsa. "I like Old Jacob."

"I love Uncle George," said Helga.

"Who doesn't!" said Elsa, catching hold of his hand and skipping along beside him as they turned into the Carlsons' yard, where Aunt Anna's bright dahlias and marigolds looked as gay as if they too were going to dance at the autumn party.

*Chapter 3*

It was still dark Tuesday morning when Grandma came to call Nancy.

"Time to get up!" she said, and lighted the gas.

Nancy opened her eyes and blinked at the light. "Is it night?" she asked, puzzled.

"No," said Grandma, "it's four o'clock in the morning and we're going to the farm."

That made Nancy come wide awake in an instant.

"It's Uncle George's idea!" she said. "But I didn't know it was going to begin early like this.

41

Are the girls here? How are we going to get to the farm? Karl the Twelfth can't . . ."

Grandma interrupted her.

"You mustn't ask any questions," she said. "What Elsa said about wanting to see all the hours of the day and night made Uncle George think of something we used to do once in a while when we were young. But we've promised not to tell you anything. You must wait and see what happens."

"Are we . . . ?" began Nancy.

"No questions!" said Grandma.

Nancy laughed. "But how can I wait!"

"Get dressed quickly and I will help you with your braids."

When they got downstairs, Aunt Hanna had a cup of warm milk ready for Nancy. "Drink this, dear," she said, "and then put on your sweater and coat. Although it's warm for September, it will be chilly so early in the morning."

"Where's Uncle George?" asked Nancy.

"No questions!" said Aunt Hanna, smiling.

Karl the Twelfth was already in the driveway, harnessed to the two-seated wagon. Grandma and Aunt Hanna got into the back seat; Oscar, Nancy, and Grandpa got in front.

"Grandpa," Nancy said, "there are so many

questions I want to ask that I don't see how I can stand it."

"Look at the morning," said Grandpa.

"It looks like night," said Nancy.

"Almost," said Grandpa, "but it will grow lighter, little by little. It will be interesting to watch."

There were no lights in any of the houses on the street.

"We are the only people who are up," said Nancy happily.

"No," said Grandpa. "Listen!"

Nancy listened. She could hear a horse and wagon.

"It's coming along East Street," said Grandpa. "We'll meet it just about as we get to the street lamp at the corner; then we can see who it is."

It was a milkman. He waved and Grandpa and Nancy waved back. Nancy lifted Oscar's paw and made him wave, too.

"That was fun," said Nancy. "Will we meet anybody else?"

"Probably not," said Grandpa, "until we get onto the road to the farm. Then we're sure to meet some of the farmers taking their milk to the early morning train."

They rode through the silent town. When they

got out into the country, the morning looked even darker, for here there were no street lights. There were lights in some of the houses, though.

"Farmers have to get up early," said Grandpa.

Sometimes, by the light of their own lantern and that from a house window, they could see a dog or a cat in a dooryard. Oscar wanted to bark a greeting to all these friends, and Grandpa had to keep saying, "No, no, Oscar. Be quiet!"

Sometimes a dog in a yard barked first and then there was no keeping Oscar still. "I am afraid we should have left you at home," Grandpa told him.

"Oh, no!" said Nancy. "He would have been so disappointed. And what would Danny have thought!"

Danny, the farm dog, and Oscar were great friends and loved to have a day together. Oscar was the one who had to do the visiting, for Danny could not be spared from the farm.

When they came to a long stretch of woods, Grandpa drew Karl the Twelfth to a stop. "We'll wait here for a few minutes and see what happens," he said.

"*Here!*" said Nancy. "In the woods?" They looked very dark and she moved a little nearer Grandpa. Soon she could hear something coming. "Is that a farmer with his milk?" she asked.

"No, I don't think so," said Grandpa. "It doesn't sound heavy enough for that. I think it's a buggy. Wait until it comes around the bend of the road and we'll see."

"It's the doctor," said Grandpa.

"Oh, dear," said Grandma. "I wonder who is sick."

But it was good news the doctor had. "A new baby at the Nelsons'," he said as he stopped by their wagon. "A fine boy."

"Is everything all right?" asked Grandma.

"It couldn't be better," said the doctor, and, after he had stayed a few minutes talking to them all, he took up the reins and signaled to his horse to move on.

"What's the baby's name?" Nancy called to him as he drove off.

"John August," he called back.

"A new baby!" said Nancy, "and we were almost right there when he came!"

"Listen again," said Grandpa. "I think this is what we're waiting for."

A wagon was coming behind them. Nancy turned around. By the lantern's light she could see that it was Uncle George and Aunt Anna and the three girls. The doctor was stopping to tell them about the new baby, too. As soon as he had waved good-by once more, they drove up beside Karl the Twelfth.

"Grandma!" called Helga. "A little new baby at the Nelsons'! I wish I could see him."

"I'll take you to see him someday soon, darling," said Grandma, "but he isn't quite ready for company yet."

"When he is old enough to understand," said Aunt Hanna, "you can say to him, 'We were driving by your house early, on the very morning you were born.' "

This delighted the children.

"Mamma, could we take him a present someday?" asked Sigrid.

"Yes, that would be nice," said Aunt Anna.

"The Nelsons have just come from Sweden," she told Uncle George and Aunt Hanna. "They bought a farm here to be near his sister and her husband who live in town. Mr. Nelson speaks English well, but she is just learning and she is very shy. She hasn't been at all well and he has been so worried about her. Martha has been to see them several times and likes them very much."

"I am so glad they have a child at last," said Grandma. "The day I went with Martha to call on Mrs. Nelson she told me they had been married for five years and wanted children so much, and had begun to be afraid they would never have any."

"That would be terrible!" said Helga. "Not to have any children!"

When the two wagons moved on again, Elsa and Oscar had changed places. She sat beside Nancy and he was on the back seat of the other wagon between Aunt Anna and Helga.

"Uncle George hired that horse from the livery stable," Elsa told Nancy, "because Karl the Twelfth couldn't carry us all. Her name is Nellie. Papa couldn't come because he has to work, but he said he has done what we are going to do and will be thinking of us. I wish he could have come, though."

"So do I!" said Nancy. "Remember when we had the birch-tree party, Grandpa had to work. It seems somebody always has to stay home."

"Papa said to remember everything to tell him," said Elsa. "Won't he be surprised when he hears about John August?"

When they came to the Nelsons' house, there were lights in every window.

"Because a little boy has come to live in it," said Nancy.

Soon after, they heard another wagon coming. This was a farmer with his milk for the train; and they met three more before they turned in at the driveway to the farm.

Uncle George was just ahead of them, and Danny and Oscar were already greeting each other. Aunt Martha had come out of the kitchen to welcome everyone. Fred Hawkins, one of the big boys who sometimes helped Uncle Sven, was carrying the new milk into the house. Through the open barn door, Nancy could see several cats drinking from the pan of milk that was always set out for them after the morning and evening milking.

Helga hurried to tell Aunt Martha about John August.

"Oh, I'm so glad," said Aunt Martha. "That's the best news I could possibly hear today! Welcome, welcome, everybody! You must be starved."

But when they got into the house the children were astonished to see that no breakfast had been set out.

"Don't take off your coats, girls," said Aunt Anna. "We're going for a walk."

"A walk!" said Helga. "Without having any . . . ?"

"Sh-hh!" said Aunt Anna.

Now Nancy saw that the grownups were taking things out of the back of Karl the Twelfth's and Nellie's wagons.

"It looks like a picnic!" she said.

"Forevermore!" said Sigrid. "What next! Ever since Uncle George and Aunt Hanna came, things have happened in a topsy-turvy way. A picnic in the dark!"

"And don't you like topsy-turvy ways?" asked Uncle George, coming up behind her.

"We *love* them," said Sigrid.

"I wish all the days were topsy-turvy days," said Elsa.

Aunt Martha came to give each of the children something to carry to the picnic. "Follow Fred," she said. "See, he has a lantern."

The children hurried after him. He led them to the field on the other side of the farmhouse and they saw that they were not going to have far to walk.

"Look!" said Elsa. "There's a light!"

"It's from a fire," said Sigrid. "It's a bonfire! We're going to have breakfast around a bonfire!"

The fire had been built on a little hill, and as they came nearer to it they could see that a man was standing there. It was Uncle Sven. He waved to them, and the children began to run. They

*49*

didn't need Fred's lantern now; the light from the fire was enough.

"I can smell coffee," said Nancy.

"You'll soon smell bacon, too," said Fred, and when they got to the fire, he took charge of frying bacon and eggs.

"How do you like this for a breakfast place, girls?" asked Uncle Sven.

"It's wonderful!" said Nancy.

"It's perfect!" said Sigrid.

"I'm hungry!" said Helga.

As soon as the grownups arrived, Grandpa and Uncle George spread blankets on the ground, and they all sat down to eat their bacon and eggs, with Grandma's homemade rye bread and butter, and mugs of hot coffee or cocoa.

"You're a great hand with the frying pan, Fred," said Uncle George. "This is a fine breakfast."

"Look over toward the east," said Grandpa, and the children turned in the direction his hand pointed.

The sky was gray now, and beginning to show color.

"I can see pale yellow," said Elsa.

"That's because the sun is coming up," said Grandpa.

"I can't see the sun, though."

"Because we're lower than the hills over there. Keep watching and soon you'll see the sun itself."

"Let's see who'll be the first one to see it coming over the hills," said Uncle George.

"Aren't we going to have any songs?" asked Nancy.

"Pretty soon," said Uncle George. "Not quite yet."

"Look," said Aunt Anna. "I can see a little pink in the sky."

"And over there it's getting brighter," said Nancy. "Everywhere it's getting lighter and lighter. Isn't it beautiful?"

"There comes the sun!" said Uncle George, and they all stood up. He and the other men took off their hats as they all began to sing, in Swedish:

"Thy glorious sun comes up once more
  As we this wonder see,
  With newborn hope and strength we sing
  Our song of praise to Thee.

"Thy sun is shining for us all.
  Help us today that we
  In love and gentle kindness may
  Grow more, Dear God, like Thee."

As they sang, the sun kept coming higher and higher over the hills. Nancy thought it was the most wonderful sight she had ever seen. When they had finished the song, they stood silent for a long time, watching the colors changing in the sky.

"I know what I'd like to sing," said Elsa suddenly. "I'd like to sing, 'My heart with rapture thrills,' because it does."

"She means 'My country, 'tis of thee,'" said Sigrid, "the part about,

"I love thy rocks and rills,
  Thy woods and templed hills.
  My heart with rapture thrills
  Like that above."

So they sang the song of Elsa's choice; and then Aunt Martha asked for "*Morgon Mellan Fjällen.*" This was a song that even Nancy knew. She could sing it in Swedish, and Grandpa had told her what the words meant. It was a great favorite with the Bensons and Carlsons.

"Morning among the mountains!
  The rivers and brooks
  Dancing over the rocks
  Sing, *God is good! God is good!*

"Now the day is breaking;
  Light comes flooding forth.

The valleys that are waking
Answer, *God is good! God is good!*"

"Our valley is waking," said Sigrid. "Look, there's Cicily-Ann Sinkspout sitting on the side piazza washing herself."

"She isn't even looking at the morning," said Nancy.

"And there's one of Wanda's brothers going out to their barn," said Aunt Anna.

They looked around the valley for a little while to see how many things they could find that were waking with the sun.

"It's so wonderful," said Sigrid.

"Let's sing the rest of the song," said Grandpa.

When the song was over, they stood silent again, looking at the sky. Danny stood beside Uncle Sven, as quiet as his family. Only Oscar was restless. At last he couldn't stand the stillness any longer. He ran from one to another of his friends, barking.

"You're right, Oscar," said Aunt Martha. "We ought to go home now. That was perfect, George! I'm so glad we came."

They were all so glad that they had to stay a little longer to tell each other how wonderful it was.

"Come on! Come on!" Oscar barked.

55

"You don't need to carry anything back, girls," said Aunt Martha.

So the four children, with Danny and Oscar ahead of them, ran down the hillside to the morning on the farm.

## Chapter 4

WEDNESDAY morning Nancy woke early, for she had gone to bed at six o'clock. She could hear Grandpa out in the yard harnessing Karl the Twelfth; and somebody moving around downstairs in the kitchen. She gave Grandma a signal they had arranged when Nancy first came. She picked up a stick that lay on the chair beside her bed and pounded on the floor. She could hear Grandma go to open the door that led to the back stairs, and in a minute Teddy came racing into her room and up onto the bed. He was always glad to have a little visit with Nancy before she got up in the morning.

"You should have come with us yesterday," she told him. "It was wonderful."

Teddy curled up beside her, purring loudly.

Nancy lay still, thinking about the lovely day at the farm, and about the little silver house, and all the things that had happened since Uncle George and Aunt Hanna came. Whoever would have thought that a visit from two grownups could be so much fun for children! She wondered what they would all do today. Maybe Grandpa would take them out to the little house again and they would see how it looked in the daytime.

When she came down to breakfast, she found that entirely different plans had been made.

"We didn't tell you children about them last night," Aunt Hanna said, "because we were afraid you'd be so excited you wouldn't sleep. You are all going visiting for a week."

"Visiting!" Nancy said in surprise. "Where?"

"Different places," said Aunt Hanna, smiling at her. "Sigrid is coming with us. You see, our daughter lives in the same town as her Grandmother Carlson, and since we're going up there for a week before we go back to Chicago we thought it would be nice to take Sigrid along. We can bring her back on our way home."

"Isn't that kind of Aunt Hanna and Uncle George?" said Grandma. "It will be lovely for Sigrid; and Grandmother Carlson will be so pleased. She gets so little chance to see the children. But that's not all the news. After that was decided, Aunt Anna said she was tempted to take advantage of this extra vacation to spend a few days with Aunt Elisabeth Carlson. She hasn't been well and things have been pretty hard for her. Helga will go with her mother; and Aunt Martha has invited you and Elsa to spend the week at the farm."

This was so much exciting news that Nancy forgot all about her oatmeal.

"Eat your breakfast," said Grandma, "and then you can come with us. We're going down to help Anna with her ironing so that she can have Sigrid ready for the afternoon train."

The Carlson girls were even more excited than Nancy was.

Sigrid's trip was, of course, the most thrilling. She had never before been away from her family or on so long a train ride as this would be.

Helga would not be going so far away and she had several times been with her family to visit

Aunt Elisabeth. Still, she wouldn't have changed places with Sigrid, for at Aunt Elisabeth's there were two little cousins—Frank, who was not quite three, and Laura, less than a year old.

"I will take care of both of them all week," said Helga happily.

Since all the children often went to the farm, going there could hardly be called a real trip; but Nancy and Elsa were perfectly satisfied. They loved the farm and to be there together for a whole week would be a special treat.

"And it's all because you had a fire in your school so you could have a vacation," Nancy said.

"And because Uncle George and Aunt Hanna came," said Sigrid.

"I will write you each a post card if I can get the time," said Helga.

"So will I," said Sigrid.

"And we will write to you," said Elsa.

"And to Alex," said Nancy. "What a lot of mail we'll all get! We'll watch for the mailman every day."

They all walked down to the afternoon train to see the first set of travelers off on their journey. It was good to know, as they waved good-by, that they would be seeing Uncle George and Aunt

Hanna again before they went back to Chicago.

The next morning Aunt Anna and Helga left, and early in the afternoon Aunt Martha came for Elsa and Nancy.

They each had a suitcase with their clothes in it, and their tiny dolls, paper dolls, crayons, pencils, and writing paper. At noontime Grandpa had stopped at the post office and bought them a little book of twelve stamps.

"I guess you won't write more than six letters each," he said.

They kissed Grandma good-by, waved to Oscar and Teddy, and drove off. It was a beautiful day. The weather had turned colder in the night, and the crisp autumn air made them all—including Whoa Emma—feel very gay.

"We have a lovely, long afternoon ahead of us," said Aunt Martha, "and I thought if you liked the idea, we'd drive out to look at your little silver house before we go to the farm."

Nothing could have pleased the little girls more.

"That will be wonderful," said Nancy. "And this time we can get out of the wagon and walk around and look at everything. Aunt Martha, do you think there might be a secret garden?"

"Probably not a walled-in one," said Aunt Martha, "but there was no doubt a garden there some time and some of the flowers may be left, though I don't think there'd be many. Still, we'll see."

Whoa Emma was always in a hurry, and now Aunt Martha had a hard time to hold her back.

"Whoa Emma, Whoa Emma!" she kept saying. "Take your time; this isn't a race."

It was no use. Whoa Emma ran as if she thought the little silver house might be on fire and she alone could save it. Nancy and Elsa were delighted; she couldn't get to the little house too soon to suit them. In no time at all, it seemed, they were there. Aunt Martha tied Whoa Emma to a good stout tree by the roadside and followed the children.

"It's beautiful!" said Nancy. "It's just as beautiful in the daytime as it was at night. Alex said it wouldn't be, but it is."

The little house did look lovely in the golden autumn sunlight. A woodbine vine with dark red leaves covered one of its gray walls. The maple tree that stood at the other side of the house was scarlet and gold. A big clump of sunny yellow flowers, called golden glow, grew by the front step.

"Do you think somebody planted the golden glows lately, Aunt Martha?" asked Nancy.

"No, I don't think so," said Aunt Martha.

"They last a long time. The ones we have at the farm must have been growing there many years; we didn't plant them. Let's look around a little and see what else we can find. I don't see how anybody could possibly mind as long as we don't touch anything."

"If only we could find one window that was not boarded up!" said Nancy.

"Or even a little crack in a board," said Elsa, "big enough to peek through. I don't know how we can stand never finding out what it's like inside!"

"Well, there certainly isn't any crack in these boards in front," said Aunt Martha. "They're very good wood, and securely fastened."

She walked around to the side where the woodbine grew, and the girls followed her. If there were any cracks in the boards here, the lovely red leaves of the woodbine hid them.

"Maybe they'd be most likely to be at the back," said Elsa.

But the back door and the windows on each side of it were securely covered.

"Only one more side," said Nancy. "Everybody wish for a crack!"

There was none. There was no way to see into the little house.

"Unless we climb up onto the roof and look down the chimney," said Nancy.

"Even that wouldn't work, I'm sure," said Aunt Martha. "The chimneys must have been closed, or birds and squirrels would get in."

Suddenly they heard a little noise above their heads, and, just as if he had heard them mentioning him, a gray squirrel leaped from the maple tree onto the roof of the little house and began to chatter at them.

"He's talking to us," said Nancy, delighted.

"I don't think he's saying anything very complimentary," said Aunt Martha. "I think he's scolding us. He probably thinks this is his property."

"Maybe it is," said Elsa. "Maybe he is enchanted; maybe he's not a squirrel at all but a person who used to live in the little house. Were you once a little boy?" she asked the squirrel, but he only stared at them.

"His squirrel name is Silver Tail," said Nancy.

"So it is," said Aunt Martha. "How did you think of it so quickly?"

"Because his tail *is* silver," said Nancy.

"And he lives at the little silver house," said Elsa.

"Oh, yes," said Nancy. "I never even thought

64

of that. Sir Silver Tail of the little silver house. I wish we had brought him some nuts."

"There are some peanuts in the grocery box in the wagon," said Aunt Martha. "I got them to put into cookies for you, but you may give a few of them to Sir Silver Tail if you'd like to."

Nancy ran to the wagon and came back with the peanuts. She knelt on the ground, held one in front of her, and looked up at Sir Silver Tail.

"Please come!" she begged. "I won't hurt you. Please!"

But Sir Silver Tail would not come.

"Leave a few on the ground," said Aunt Martha, "and maybe he'll come and get them. Let's go see if we can find any trace of a garden."

"Oh, I do hope there is one," said Nancy.

"If I were going to plant a garden," Aunt Martha said, "I think I'd choose that piece of land over there at the left. See, where that tall grass is!"

They walked in the direction she pointed. Nancy ran on ahead.

"It's not just grass here, Aunt Martha!" she said. "There's something else, too."

Aunt Martha knew so much about gardens that she could tell from the brown and withering leaves what flowers had grown there.

"Mignonette," she said, "and verbena and calendulas and little pinks. And look, Nancy! I do believe your favorite flower of all is here!"

"Not a yellow rosebush!" said Nancy.

"I think so," said Aunt Martha. "Of course I can't be really sure, but the leaves look like those the little old-fashioned, sweet yellow roses have. Like the bush Mrs. Hackett has from England. We can't know for certain until spring, of course."

"Oh, I can hardly wait to see!" said Nancy, and then added suddenly, "But I won't be here. I won't be here to see the yellow rosebush."

"Oh, *dear!*" said Elsa.

They both looked so troubled that Aunt Martha said quickly, "But you'll come to visit us sometime."

"Not when yellow roses bloom," said Nancy. "Not in June. I'll be in school always in June."

"Come, come," said Aunt Martha. "We mustn't stand here on the first day of October worrying about the middle of June—especially about not seeing yellow roses on a bush that may not be a yellow rosebush after all. We sound like The Three Sillies! Let's see what else we can find."

She knelt on the ground and began to push away some of the leaves.

"Look, girls," she said, "here's something still in blossom. Little ladies' delights!"

The children hurried to see.

"They look like tiny pansies," said Nancy.

"They are cousins to our garden pansies," said Aunt Martha. "Some people call them wild pansies."

"I've seen them before," said Elsa. "My teacher had some in school once. She called them heartsease."

"Yes, I've heard them called that, too," said Aunt Martha.

"Goodness!" said Nancy. "Three names!"

"I know two more," said Aunt Martha, laughing. "I never realized before how many names this little flower has. Viola is one and Johnny-jump-up is another."

"Johnny-jump-up!" said Nancy. "Aunt Martha, could we pick a little bouquet for John August? Tiny, tiny Johnny-jump-ups for a tiny, tiny baby?"

"Oh, no, we mustn't," said Aunt Martha. "They don't belong to us. We mustn't touch anything."

The girls realized that she was right.

"It would be awful if everybody came picking things here," said Nancy. "But it would have been just right for a baby."

"Well, there's a garden all right," said Aunt Martha, "even if it's not a secret one. In a way it's secret, though, because we don't know what we might find if we could dig around a bit."

"I wish we could," said Nancy. "I'd love it more than anything."

"So would I," said Aunt Martha, "but we certainly can't go digging up other people's gardens no matter how much we want to; and we'd better be getting back to the farm. I've got things I must do, and you'll want to get unpacked and settled. I'm glad we came, though."

"Could we come again, do you think," asked Elsa, "and walk down through the field to the woods? I'd like to see if there's a brook."

"Maybe we can," said Aunt Martha. "I want to speak to Uncle Sven about it, though. The more I think about it, the more I'm not sure we ought to be walking on this property at all. Even if nobody lives on the land, it does belong to somebody."

"But we love it so!" said Nancy.

They walked back to the little house. The peanuts were gone and so was Silver Tail.

"Anyway, I'm glad he got them," said Elsa.

They stopped once more to look at the wood-bine and the maple tree and the golden glow flowers.

"It's so beautiful," said Nancy. "It's so sad to leave it."

They got into the wagon and Aunt Martha headed Whoa Emma toward home. As Nancy turned back to wave good-by to the little house, she had a surprise.

"Look! Quick!" she cried. "There's a boy!" But even before Aunt Martha and Elsa could turn around, he had disappeared.

"He was standing near the maple tree," said Nancy, "right beside the little house, but when I called to you, he ran. Who do you suppose he was?"

"Probably some boy out exploring because it's vacation," said Aunt Martha. "How did he look?"

"I don't know exactly," said Nancy, "because I saw him so little. He was about ten, I guess, and he had on overalls and a sweater and he was look-ing *hard* at us. Oh, dear, I hope he doesn't do any-thing to hurt the little house."

"Did he look like that kind of boy?" asked Elsa.

"No, I don't think so," said Nancy. "I don't know. But there seems to be so much to worry about—about a house—fire, and what people might do to it, and everything! Oh, Aunt Martha, we'll *have* to come back."

"Maybe the boy lives near here and goes to the house often and could tell us about it," said Elsa. "We could at least drive by the house to see if we see him again. It wouldn't be against the law just to drive by."

"No, that's true," said Aunt Martha, laughing. "We'll try to come back and I think I can make time."

It never took Whoa Emma long to get wherever she was going, so it was only a little after three when they reached the farm. Danny came running to meet them; Uncle Sven came to unharness Whoa Emma; and Aunt Martha and the girls went into the house.

When all four girls came to the farm to stay overnight, they slept in the big open attic so they could be together. But now Aunt Martha picked up the two suitcases and led Nancy and Elsa to the best spare room.

"I thought you might like to sleep here," she said, "since there are only two of you."

"It will seem as if we were real grown-up ladies

come visiting," said Elsa. "I'm glad we brought our jewels."

"I'll leave you to do your unpacking," said Aunt Martha, "and by the time you've finished I'll have cocoa ready for you downstairs."

"We can each have one big bureau drawer and one small one," said Nancy, "and half the jewel box."

They loved the jewel box which stood on the bureau. It was made of wood, and it had been in the farmhouse when Uncle Sven bought it. The box was painted a shiny black and the bottom of it was lined with rose-colored velvet. The box had a lovely smell; Aunt Martha said it was sandalwood.

"And we can each have half the closet," said Elsa, opening the door. "I love the smell in here, too."

So did Nancy. It came from a kind of dried grass called "sweet grass." Aunt Martha always kept a bunch of it in the closet, and it made whatever else was in there smell sweet, too.

"Let's unpack our jewels first," said Elsa.

Her "jewels" were a string of blue beads and a little gold pin with a tiny red stone in it. Nancy's were a fine gold chain with a locket, and a silver link bracelet with a tiny heart attached to it. They would probably not wear any of these things while they were at the farm.

"Still, you should always take your jewels when you go traveling," said Elsa, "and they will look nice in the jewel box."

The blue beads looked especially pretty against the softly faded rose velvet.

"I'm going to put my underclothes and aprons and hair ribbons and things like that in the big drawer, and my writing paper and pencils and desk kind of things in the small drawer," said Elsa.

"That's a good idea," said Nancy. "That's what I'll do, too. But where shall we put Trillium and Jasmine and all their things?"

"Oh, I know," she answered herself. "We could leave our suitcases open on the floor of the closet, and the dolls can each have a suitcase for a house and keep all their things in it. And we could maybe get some cardboard or something and make some little tables and chairs and beds."

"That's a wonderful idea," said Elsa. "Their address can be Sweet Grass Lane and they can give a party and invite Violet and Wanda. Won't we have fun?"

"All kinds of fun!" said Nancy. "Let's hurry to get our things put away."

"Cocoa!" called Aunt Martha, just as they finished; and they ran downstairs to begin their unexpected vacation at the farm.

*Chapter* 5

THAT was a lovely week. Nancy had thought no season at the farm could be so beautiful as the springtime when the apple trees and lilacs were in blossom, and, a little later, the fields grew white and gold with daisies and buttercups. But now the autumn seemed in some ways just as lovely.

It was October and almost every day was crisp and clear. Elsa's class in school had begun to learn a poem about it:

> Oh, suns and skies and clouds of June,
> And flowers of June together,

You cannot rival for one hour
October's bright blue weather.

"Well, I don't know," said Nancy. "I love the bright blue weather, but June has the roses."

"The red apples on the trees are just as pretty," said Elsa. "And I love the smell of the wild grapes and they are royal purple! And the leaves!"

Nancy had to agree that it would be hard to find anything lovelier than the leaves, especially the maple leaves. They were yellow and gold and green and scarlet. On their first afternoon at the farm, she and Elsa raked together piles of them, just for the fun of running through them and even rolling over and over in them. They looked at the leaves, too.

"Let's see how many we can find that are alike," said Elsa.

They hunted and hunted, but they couldn't find even two that were exactly alike. They might be almost alike, but not exactly. It was amazing.

"We must have handled hundreds of leaves," Nancy told Aunt Martha.

"You could have handled thousands," said Aunt Martha, "and the same thing would have been true. I have read that there are no two things exactly alike in this whole wonderful world of ours."

"Think of all the maple trees in all the world," said Elsa, "and no two leaves alike!"

Aunt Martha had invited Wanda to come to supper; and after supper she built a fire in the fireplace. This was a special treat. None of the girls had fireplaces at home; their houses had only stoves.

"I could sit for hours, I think, looking at an open fire," said Aunt Martha. "I couldn't sit and look right at a lamp or at the sun, but the light of a fire never seems to make my eyes tired."

About seven o'clock Wanda's father came over, and he and Uncle Sven sat by the fire, too, and talked about the time when they were boys— Uncle Sven in Sweden, and Wanda's father in Poland. The children wanted to sit up late, but Wanda had to go to school the next day. She went to the little country school at the foot of the hill and she wasn't having a vacation. She was especially busy because the school was preparing a play for Thanksgiving, and Wanda had the leading part. Such an important person had to go to bed early.

After she and her father had gone, Aunt Martha let Nancy and Elsa sit by the fire a little longer, and then she sent them up to bed.

"We'll have more fires while you're here," she said.

"Let's tell each other stories after we get into bed," said Elsa.

But it had been an exciting day and they had been outdoors in the autumn air a long time. Before they even began a story they were fast asleep.

The kitten, Cuckoo Clock, woke them in the morning. She came bounding onto the bed just as Teddy did at Grandma's. But she didn't want to settle down quietly as he always did. She was a much younger cat and she wanted to play.

"She's got something around her neck," said Elsa.

"I think it's a note," said Nancy, catching Cuckoo Clock and trying to hold her still long enough to untie the ribbon around which the note was twisted.

"I'll hold her while you untie it," said Elsa. "You're not a very good mailman," she told the kitten. "You ought to let us have our letter."

"I've got it," said Nancy. She unfolded the paper, and together they read the letter:

78

Get up quick!
Letters to write. Dumplings to make.
Nuts to get ready for butternut fudge.
And a book you've never read.

"A new book and butternut fudge! Let's hurry," said Elsa, jumping out of bed with Cuckoo Clock dashing after her as if this were some kind of game.

The girls dressed quickly and ran downstairs. They ate their breakfast, washed and wiped the dishes, and made their bed.

"Run out and play a little while," said Aunt Martha, "and then come in to do some of your letter writing. We'll have to save the book and the butternuts for the afternoon. Let's see, this is Friday. If you get something ready for the mailman to take this afternoon, Sigrid and Helga and Alex will get it by Monday. They'll probably be starting home Tuesday or Wednesday."

"My goodness!" said Elsa. "Vacation goes fast. We'll come in right after we've had a good run in the leaves. I don't suppose we'll get any mail ourselves this afternoon, but we'll go look anyway when it's time."

"I'm waiting for a package," said Aunt Martha, "and it should come any day now. My bulbs."

Nancy and Elsa knew how long Aunt Martha

had wanted these bulbs. Up to this time, she had raised all her flowers from seeds. But you had to have bulbs if you wanted flowers like tulips and hyacinths, crocuses and daffodils, which were planted in the fall and blossomed in the spring. And bulbs cost much more than seeds. At last she had saved enough money from the eggs she sold to send for the bulbs.

Nancy was thrilled to think they might come while she and Elsa were at the farm.

"May we help you plant them?" she said.

"Yes, indeed," said Aunt Martha.

"Let's walk way up the road to the end of the field where the big maple trees are," said Nancy, "and play in the leaves there."

As they walked along, they talked about their letters.

"We have six stamps each," said Elsa. "We'll each write to Sigrid, Alex, and Helga."

"I want to write to Mamma and Papa, too," said Nancy, "but I don't need to use the stamps for them because Papa sent me some stamped, addressed envelopes all ready to use. So we'll each have three stamps left. Shall we write to Grandma and Grandpa?"

"We'll be seeing them Sunday," said Elsa, "but I guess maybe they'd like to get some mail anyway. And I want to write to Mamma and Papa. And I think we should use only five stamps each and save one each for an emergency."

"An emergency?" said Nancy. "What kind of an emergency?"

"Oh, I don't know," said Elsa, "but something unexpected might come up. Or else we should each write one surprising letter to somebody who doesn't expect to hear from us. To somebody we don't even know, or something like that. I'll think of something. Oh, and we want to write to Uncle George and Aunt Hanna."

"I know what," said Nancy. "You use one stamp for your mother and one for your father; and I'll use one of mine for Grandpa and Grandma together, and one for Uncle George and Aunt Hanna. Mr. and Mrs., you know; people often do that. And we can write those letters together."

"That's a good idea," said Elsa. "And one of us can tell Alex and Sigrid and Helga about the little house; and the other one can tell about what we're doing on the farm."

So that was all planned, and they began to run. They played in the leaves until Aunt Martha called them by ringing the big cowbell she kept on the kitchen porch.

"M-m-m, smells good!" said Elsa, as they came running into the kitchen.

"Beef stew," said Aunt Martha. "After you've written your letters, we'll make the dumplings to go in it."

"Good," said Elsa. "I love dumplings."

"So do I," said Nancy.

They ran upstairs to get their writing paper and stamps.

"Bring your aprons down, too," said Aunt Martha.

They settled themselves at the kitchen table and began their letters. It took much longer to write them than to plan them.

"If I were you," said Aunt Martha, "I'd write only to the children today, and to the grownups tomorrow."

"Let's," said Nancy. "Then we can go out to mail the letters and have a run with Danny before we make the dumplings. There's always so much to do on a farm that time goes too fast."

Making the dumplings was fun. First Nancy and Elsa washed their hands and put on their aprons. These were new aprons and very pretty. Aunt Anna had made one for each of her little

girls, and one for Nancy. At Elsa's request
had copied the pattern of Alice's apron in *A*
*in Wonderland*. All four were made alike, but
were different colors. Elsa's was light green and
Nancy's pale yellow.

Aunt Martha helped them mix the dough for
the dumplings and then they took turns dropping
it from a big spoon into the hot stew. At dinner
time Uncle Sven said they were the best dumplings
he had ever tasted.

"I like this kind of vacation," said Elsa.

The afternoon was especially interesting.

"I'm going to make butternut fudge tomorrow
or Monday," said Aunt Martha. "If you'd like to
help get the butternuts ready, I'll build a fire in
the fireplace and read aloud to you while you pick
out the nut meats. I got a book at the library for
you. It is *Mary's Meadow* by Juliana Horatia
Ewing, and I'm pretty sure you'll like it. But it
has some unusual names and long words in it, and
I think you'll enjoy it more when you read it
yourselves if you've heard it first."

The girls were delighted; they loved to be read
to. Fudge and a fire and a new story to hear—all
this would be more than worth the hard work of
getting the butternuts ready.

Butternuts were so hard-shelled that Uncle

*83*

Sven cracked them with a tool called a vise. But that was only the beginning; after that the nut meats had to be pried out of the shells with a nut-pick. It was almost impossible to get the nuts out whole, but that didn't matter because they would be chopped into small pieces for the fudge, anyway.

Aunt Martha's butternut fudge was famous among all her neighbors and her friends in town. She made it only once or twice a year, but when she did she made a great deal of it. This is the way she always did it.

She put a big iron kettle on the kitchen stove. Into the kettle she poured rich cream and maple syrup. "How much of each?" people would ask her. Aunt Martha could not tell them. "Oh, just enough to make it come out right," she would say, "I never measure it." "And how long do you cook it?" someone might ask. "Until it's ready," was all Aunt Martha could answer.

When it had cooked a long time, very slowly, Aunt Martha put in the butternuts, beat it with a big spoon, and poured it into pans to harden. It didn't seem to matter that she didn't know exactly how she did it. It always came out right. It was the best fudge anybody had ever tasted.

The girls took a pan of butternuts and a bowl

and a nutpick each, and sat down on the floor in front of the fire. Aunt Martha sat near them in a rocking chair. Nancy and Elsa could tell almost as soon as she began to read that they were going to like *Mary's Meadow*.

Mary in the book loved flowers as much as Nancy did. She and her brothers and sister thought it would be wonderful to make the whole world into a beautiful garden. They decided they would begin by planting flowers along the roadside and in waste places where nobody would ever expect to find them growing. While they were doing this, they did not call each other by their ordinary names; each one chose a special name. Mary's was Traveler's Joy. The book told about their adventures.

"Oh, that's a good book," said Elsa when Aunt Martha stopped reading to rest her voice a few minutes.

"It's the most wonderful idea I ever heard of," said Nancy. "Why didn't we have the book this spring? Then all spring and summer the Crimson Rambler Club could have planted flowers along the roadsides. Traveler's Joy! It would be better for a club to do than have a show or a fair or anything. But we can't do it in the winter, and next spring I won't be here."

"Don't talk about not being here, *please*," said Elsa. "I can't bear to think about it."

Nancy couldn't bear to think about it either. Of course, she wanted to go back to her mother and father. There were days when it seemed to her she couldn't wait until her mother was well, so that she could be with them again. But she was having such a good time with the Bensons and Carlsons, and with Alex and his mother, that she didn't see how she could get along without them, either. Think of not having Elsa to play with any more!

It was better not to think about it; and it was lucky that Cuckoo Clock came in just then, dragging a ball of yarn behind her. When Aunt Martha tried to get it away from her, Cuckoo Clock rolled over and over until she was all tangled in the yarn, and Nancy and Elsa had to help get her loose. There was no time to think of your own troubles when Cuckoo Clock was around. She got into more mischief than any cat on the farm. After they had finally untangled her, Aunt Martha went on with the reading.

*Mary's Meadow* grew more and more interesting. Aunt Martha read until a little before four o'clock; then she put the book down.

"It's almost time for the mailman," she said.

"You'd better take a little time off and go outdoors and watch for him. If he brings the bulbs, I'll come down to get them."

The mailbox for the farm was at the end of the driveway. About four o'clock every afternoon except Sunday the mailman came by. He rode in a buggy and drove a large white horse. If he put any mail in the box, he raised the red tin flag on the edge of it. Usually the children waited by the window to see if he put the flag up. But when anything as exciting as bulbs might be coming, it was better to be right there.

Danny went with the children. Some dogs barked at the mailman and worried his horse, but Danny had more sense. He liked the mailman and if he wasn't busy with Uncle Sven somewhere else on the farm, he always went down the driveway to greet his friend. It didn't make any difference to Danny whether there was any mail or not.

Today there was mail.

"A big package for Miss Martha Benson," the mailman said. "I'll have to get it out of the back of the wagon."

"It's bulbs," Elsa told him. "They're going to be tulips and crocuses and hyacinths and daffodils."

"Is that so?" he answered. "You don't mean to

tell me I'm carrying a whole garden in this box!"

"Yes, you are!" said Nancy, delighted. "A whole garden!"

"Aunt Martha has been saving a long time to buy them," said Elsa. "Did you know that you can get hundreds of flowers from one five-cent package of seeds? But one of these bulbs that grows into one tulip costs about five cents. So you can see it takes a long time to save for them."

"I should say so," said the mailman, setting the box on the ground. "Can you carry this up to the house?"

"Aunt Martha's coming to get it," said Elsa. "Is there any other mail?"

"Only Danny's paper," said the mailman.

He always called the newspaper which came on Friday "Danny's paper," because Danny carried it up to the house. If there was no other mail on Friday, the mailman didn't have to put up the flag.

"Here you are, my friend," he said, throwing the paper, and Danny caught it in his mouth.

"We're expecting some mail while we're here," said Nancy.

"I'll be on the lookout for it," said the mailman, and drove away.

Aunt Martha was already coming down the driveway. She picked up the box of bulbs and, with Danny and the children dancing along beside her, walked back to the house.

"Even Danny's excited," said Nancy.

"Yes," said Aunt Martha, "he always seems to know when his family is especially happy or sad."

"It's tulips, Danny," Nancy told him, "and daffodils and hyacinths and little tiny crocuses. Aunt Martha, the mailman said there is a whole flower garden in that box."

"So there is," said Aunt Martha. "Just think, we'll put the bulbs down in the cold ground, and in the spring they'll come up into beautiful flowers. I have never had any bulb garden except that little row of red tulips Mrs. Hackett so kindly gave me last year. And I've always wanted one. But it seemed as if every time I'd save enough to buy some bulbs, something would happen to make me have to spend the money for something else. This time I hurried up and sent in the order and the money before anything could happen!

"I suppose I was extravagant; but, anyway, here they are at last, and tomorrow we'll plant them."

*Chapter 6*

SATURDAY was a cold and rainy day.

"This is not a good day to plant bulbs," Aunt Martha said. "We'll make the butternut fudge this afternoon, instead, and be free to do our planting on Monday. While the fudge is cooking, we'll finish reading *Mary's Meadow*."

Nancy and Elsa found plenty to do in the morning. They washed the dishes, made their bed, and wrote the rest of their letters. They put on their coats and hats and rubbers, borrowed Uncle Sven's big umbrella, and walked down to the mailbox. When they got back, they brought down to the kitchen the cardboard and pieces of cloth Aunt Martha had found for them and began to make the furniture for the suitcase houses on Sweet Grass Lane.

About eleven o'clock the front doorbell rang. This was very unusual. Hardly anyone used the front door at the farmhouse. People almost always came up the driveway to the side piazza.

"Who in the world can that be?" said Aunt Martha.

She went into the front hall, and the girls, full of curiosity, followed her. Aunt Martha opened the door. There on the step sat a drenched and bedraggled-looking little cat!

"Cuckoo Clock!" said Aunt Martha.

"Could *she* ring the doorbell?" said Nancy.

They looked up and down the road. There was no one else in sight.

"I suppose she could have," said Aunt Martha, "but I never before heard of a cat who rang doorbells."

The bell on the farmhouse door was an old-fashioned one. It looked like a little handle. When you turned this handle, it made the bell ring.

"I suppose if she wanted to get in," said Aunt

Martha, "she might clamber up on the door and turn the handle by accident—it turns easily."

"I think she did it on purpose!" said Elsa.

Cuckoo Clock had run into the house while they were talking and was now lapping milk from her saucer near the kitchen stove.

The children were so eager to tell Uncle Sven what a remarkable cat she was that they stood watching for him at the kitchen window until he came in to dinner.

"Cuckoo Clock rang the doorbell!" said Elsa.

Uncle Sven was as much surprised as they had been, but when he had thought about the matter a little while, he said, "I suppose you could teach a cat to ring the bell."

"How?" asked the girls.

"You could tie a little something she likes to eat onto the bell and let her smell it. She'd climb up to get it all right. Then one of you could open the door from the inside. If you did it a few times, she might realize that touching the handle of the bell had something to do with the door opening for her. I don't know if it would work; but you could try it. That is, if Martha doesn't mind bothering with a cat who won't use the side door."

Aunt Martha laughed. "I wouldn't mind," she said. "It would be quite a distinction to have a cat who rang the front doorbell. I guess if sometime it wasn't convenient for me to go to the front door, she'd come around the side way fast enough, if she really wanted to get in."

The girls decided they would begin that afternoon to teach Cuckoo Clock this trick.

"She went out to the barn as soon as she'd finished drinking her milk," said Aunt Martha. "Lately she seems to like to curl up in the hay when she wants a nap. If it's not too wet when she comes in again, you can begin to teach her. If it's still raining, you'd better wait until tomorrow."

They had not even finished their dessert before they learned that Cuckoo Clock did not need any teachers.

The front doorbell rang again!

Nancy and Elsa hurried to the door. There sat Cuckoo Clock waiting to get in.

Nobody would ever know why she had suddenly decided to use this door. Neither could anybody tell whether she realized that it was the sound of the bell that made people come to let her in. Perhaps she just used the little handle as something to get hold of when she wanted to scramble up on the door to attract attention.

"It surely is lucky," Elsa told her, "that we

gave you such an unusual name. You are a very unusual cat."

When dinner was over and the dishes were done, Aunt Martha got out her biggest iron kettle and poured in the heavy cream and maple syrup. It was a good thing that Uncle Sven's cows gave rich milk and that there were plenty of butternut and maple trees on the farm. She could not have afforded to make the fudge if she had had to buy all the material for it in the stores.

"It looks like an awful lot," said Nancy.

"It's not so much as I wish we could make," said Aunt Martha. "I want to send some back to Chicago with Uncle George and Aunt Hanna. And, of course, you and Elsa must have some to take home. And I want to give some to Alex and his mother and to Wanda's family and John August's. And I thought maybe you'd like to send a little box of it to your father, Nancy. I'm afraid your mother can't have any in the hospital. I'll make some for her when she is well again. Anyway, you see even as big a kettle as this won't hold too much."

"Especially since it's the best fudge in the world," said Elsa.

Aunt Martha took *Mary's Meadow* from the shelf and sat down in a rocking chair by the stove.

Cicily-Ann Sinkspout jumped into her lap and settled herself comfortably. Nancy and Elsa sat by the kitchen table; they planned to work on their furniture while Aunt Martha read. But they soon put down their scissors and paste. They forgot all about Sweet Grass Lane and the suitcase houses. They didn't even notice that the rain had stopped and the sun come out. Their thoughts were all with the children in *Mary's Meadow*.

From time to time Aunt Martha picked up her long wooden spoon and stirred the fudge; but she sat back in her chair again immediately and hardly interrupted her reading. When at last she finished the story, Nancy sighed.

"That's the best, best book I ever read," she said.

"And *wouldn't* it be a good thing for a club to do?" said Elsa.

"It would be better than anything," said Nancy.

"It *would* be fun," said Aunt Martha.

There was a knock at the door.

"Good gracious!" said Aunt Martha. "Has Cuckoo Clock learned how to knock, too?"

This time it was not Cuckoo Clock. It was Anton, one of Wanda's older brothers, with a plate covered with a napkin. He handed the plate to Aunt Martha.

"My mother sent it over," he said. "It's a kind of Polish cake. She made it and she thought you and the girls might like a little this afternoon. Wanda had to go to the schoolhouse to practice for the play." Nancy and Elsa looked at the cake with interest.

"It looks wonderful," said Elsa.

"Your mother is very kind," said Aunt Martha. "We'll have it for a treat as soon as the fudge is done, and that will be in a few minutes. Would you like to stay long enough, Anton, to be one of the kettle scrapers? I'll leave enough in the kettle so you can all three have a taste."

"Yes, I would," said Anton. "I'll go and get your mail while I'm waiting. The flag is up."

They had been so much interested in *Mary's Meadow* that they had even forgotten the mail. Anton brought back letters for Nancy and Elsa from Sigrid. Elsa read hers aloud:

"The first night I was homesick. I cried. But now I'm having fun. Tomorrow I'm going to a club meeting of girls in Grandmother's church. It is a sewing club. They are making things for a Thanksgiving fair. I wish the Crimson Rambler Club could have a fair. We went to see Aunt

Hanna's daughter. She has three boys and no girls. They have bicycles. Johnny let me ride on his handle bars. Love, Sigrid."

"My goodness, they must be rich," said Elsa. "Three children in the family and still money enough for each one to have a bicycle."

Nancy's letter said:

"Have you found out any more about the little silver house? You would like my Grandmother Carlson's house. Her sitting room is like a garden. I counted the plants in it. She has forty-seven. Twenty are in blossom. I help water them. I am making an apron for the fair the girls' sewing club is having. Grandmother gave me the cloth. It is red and white. The apron will be for a little girl. Love, Sigrid."

"I'd like to see Grandmother Carlson's house," said Nancy. "When I grow up and have a house of my own, I'll have a sitting room that's like a garden. Sigrid writes good letters."

"Yes, she does," said Aunt Martha. "She has told us interesting things."

Now the fudge was ready for the butternuts. Aunt Martha put them in, and Anton helped her to beat it. It was heavy work to beat so much fudge. After it had been poured into pans to cool, the three children scraped the kettle.

"It *is* the best fudge in the world," said Nancy. "You were right, Elsa."

While they were eating their Polish cake, they told Anton about Cuckoo Clock. He was surprised, too. Everybody was surprised to hear about a cat who could ring a doorbell.

"She'd make a good Halloween cat," said Anton.

After supper, while Nancy and Elsa sat reading by the fire, Nancy jumped up suddenly.

"I've just had the most wonderful idea," she said. "Let's go tell Aunt Martha."

With Elsa following her, she dashed off to the kitchen.

"Aunt Martha," she said, "would there be time to send for more bulbs?"

"More bulbs?" asked Aunt Martha, puzzled. "We don't need any more bulbs."

"I have twenty-five cents here," said Nancy, "and a little money in my pig bank. If I could use it all to buy some bulbs, could we plant them in the garden of the little silver house?"

"Oh, Nancy!" said Elsa. "How wonderful! I've got twenty-five cents, too, and maybe Mamma would let me open my bank. Aunt Martha, wouldn't it be exciting to plant bulbs in the little house garden and have them come up in the spring! Everybody'd be so surprised."

"It would make it a kind of secret garden," said Nancy. "Aunt Martha, please!"

Aunt Martha looked troubled.

"It isn't our garden, children," she said. "We can't go planting things in other people's gardens."

"But, Aunt Martha," said Elsa, "it isn't a bit like *taking* something from a garden. It would be *giving* it something to make it more beautiful. That can't be wrong."

"Oh, dear," said Aunt Martha. "I wish I could say that it would be all right to do it, but I can't. I hate to disappoint you, because it was a good idea, Nancy, and it would have been fun."

To her surprise, and Elsa's, Nancy didn't look disappointed at all.

"Never mind," she said. "I know what we can do. We can plant the bulbs by the roadside near the little silver house. Not in the garden, but by the roadside the way the children do in *Mary's Meadow*. For a surprise. For Traveler's Joy!"

"For Traveler's Joy!" said Elsa. "Of course! Nobody would care if we planted them by the roadside."

Aunt Martha did not answer at once, but presently she smiled.

"No," she said, "I don't think it would do any

harm to put in a few surprise bulbs by the road-side. If anybody comes along and sees us doing it, they'll wonder what's the matter with us. But never mind that. We'll do it!"

"May we write for the bulbs this very night?" asked Elsa. "But—what if they don't get here in time?"

"I'm afraid they wouldn't," said Aunt Martha, "but I know what we can do. I sent for ten dozen —that's one hundred and twenty bulbs. No wonder I feel extravagant. I'll . . ."

She stopped suddenly and looked at the children, so eager to do something for the little house.

"I tell you," she went on, "I'll sell you each twenty-five cents' worth of bulbs, and we'll plant them some day next week. How will that be?"

"Oh, Aunt Martha," said Nancy. "You're so *good*."

"You should have the same name as Mary," said Elsa. "You should be called Traveler's Joy."

"May we get our twenty-five cents and buy the bulbs tonight?" asked Nancy. "That will be five bulbs for each of us, won't it?"

"Well," said Aunt Martha, "since it's for the little silver house, I'll give you a bargain price. We'll keep one hundred bulbs here for the farm, and plant twenty for Traveler's Joy."

"It's lucky we all went on trips this week," said Elsa, "so Papa gave us each twenty-five cents to spend. I never got twenty-five whole cents all at once, before, in my life. They certainly came in handy."

Monday was another clear blue day.

"This is good planting weather," said Aunt Martha. "Who knows what it will be tomorrow? We'll plant the bulbs here at the farm this morning and go to the little house this afternoon. The washing can wait until Tuesday, for once."

"In topsy-turvy weeks like this," said Nancy, "you ought not to do the washing on the right day, anyway."

"You ought to be really topsy-turvy," said Elsa, "and iron your clothes first and wash them afterward."

"No, thank you!" said Aunt Martha. "We're acting quite topsy-turvy enough as it is!"

"Perhaps that's why Cuckoo Clock went to the front door and rang the doorbell," said Elsa. "She knew it would be a topsy-turvy kind of thing for a cat to do."

It was fun to help plant the bulb garden at the farm in the morning and to cover it with a blanket of leaves to keep it warm until the snow came.

But the girls knew that the afternoon would be much more exciting; and they were fairly brimming over with happiness when they set out. At last it seemed to them that they were really going to do something for the little silver house.

They found that frost had killed the golden glow flowers, and the maple tree had lost most of its leaves. The little house looked sad and lonely.

"It will be so cold this winter," said Nancy, "without any fires in it."

"And at Christmas," said Elsa, "it won't have any tree or any candles in the windows. Poor little house!"

"It is sad," said Aunt Martha, "but it won't help to stand and worry about it. We must do our planting and, who knows, maybe we can think of something else to do another time. Come along."

It was easy to plant bulbs in the soil of Aunt Martha's garden; it was more difficult to do it here by the side of the road where the ground was hard. Aunt Martha had brought a sharp trowel, but it took a long time to dig the holes anyway. They didn't mind, though, because they knew how surprised people were going to be next spring when they came along the road and suddenly saw purple hyacinths and yellow daffodils, and a few bright tulips where they never would have expected such flowers to grow.

They were working so hard that they did not notice the boy coming down the road until he was standing beside them. Elsa saw him first.

"Hi!" she said. "Are you the boy Nancy saw? This is my Aunt Martha and I'm Elsa Carlson and this is Nancy Bruce. What's your name?"

"Ben Emmons," said the boy. "What are you doing here?"

Aunt Martha looked at Ben and saw at once how unhappy he was. She made a quick decision.

"You'll never guess, Ben," she said; and, turning to the girls, she added, "I think since Ben has come and caught us we'd better tell him our secret, don't you?"

Her eyes said more than that to Nancy and Elsa, and they nodded. So Aunt Martha told Ben a little about the story of *Mary's Meadow*, and why they had come to plant the flowers near the little house.

"Do you think it's a good idea?" she asked.

"I guess so," said Ben, "but I don't think anything is good in the country. I *hate* it."

"You hate the country!" said Nancy. "But how can you?"

"Because there's nothing to do," said Ben, "and in the city there's always something going on."

"We must finish our planting," said Aunt Martha, "and then we'll have a little party. I brought some gingerbread because I knew we'd be hungry after working so hard. There's plenty for you, too, Ben, and while we're eating, perhaps you'll tell us a little about the city. Nancy is the only one of us who knows anything about it. Elsa and I have never seen a big city. But, first, we must get on with our work."

"I could help dig," said Ben.

"Good!" answered Aunt Martha, and handed him the trowel.

Elsa and Nancy wanted to know all about Ben, especially how he happened to be at the little silver house.

"Because there isn't any other place to go," said Ben. "I've just come to live with the Taylors down the road."

"Is Mr. Taylor the caretaker of this house?" asked Nancy.

"Yes."

"Are they your uncle and aunt or something?" asked Elsa. "Or how did you happen to come to live with them?"

"I lived with my grandmother," Ben answered.

"She's old and she isn't able to work any longer, and so she had to go to an old people's home. I know I could have worked to take care of her but they wouldn't let me. They said I had to go to school. My grandmother knows some people who know the Taylors, and knew they wanted a boy to come to live with them to help with the work, and so they sent me here. I want to earn some money as soon as I can, so I can go back to the city and take care of my grandmother."

"Are the Taylors cruel to you?" asked Elsa sympathetically.

"Oh, no, they're all right. There just isn't anything to do."

"I thought you were going to help them," said Nancy.

"They think I need to get strong first," said Ben. "They don't think I look well. But really I'm awfully strong. They say to stay outdoors and play until school opens again; they said it closed because of a fire. They say every day to go out and play; and there isn't anything to *do!*"

"You must be going to the town school," said Nancy. "How are you going to get there?"

"Mr. Taylor works in town. He takes care of people's yards and gardens and furnaces, and I'm going to ride with him."

"I know how you feel," said Nancy. "Last April my mother had to go to the hospital. That's why I'm staying at the Bensons'. At first I was terribly lonesome, but now I love the country—much more than the city—and I think you will, too, as soon as you get used to it."

"And now you've got some friends," said Elsa. "You'll be going to the same school I do and I'll look for you the day it opens."

"And you must come to visit us at the farm someday," said Aunt Martha, "and get acquainted with all the animals."

"And to see us in town, too," said Elsa, "and get to know Alex."

Ben seemed so bewildered by all these plans that were being made for him that Aunt Martha said, "Girls, we must stop talking now or we'll never finish our planting. Not another word from any of us until the work is done!"

When the last bulb had been put into the ground, and covered with earth and leaves, Aunt Martha went to the buggy and took out a can of water and some old towels.

"Let's see if we can get our hands reasonably clean before we have our gingerbread," she said.

"Where shall we sit for our picnic?" asked Nancy.

"I think we'd better stand up," said Aunt Martha. "There's not a good place here for a sitting-down picnic."

"If it would be all right to spread that big blanket in the wagon down on the ground, then we could sit in the yard," said Ben.

"I don't believe we'd better do that, Ben," said Aunt Martha. "It's not our yard, you know."

"Mr. Taylor said I could play in the yard and the woods as long as I didn't destroy anything," said Ben. "He wouldn't care if we sat on the ground."

"Please, Aunt Martha," said Elsa.

"Well, since Ben is sure it's all right, we'll do it this one time," said Aunt Martha.

She and Ben spread the horse blanket on the ground; and they all sat down near the wall with the woodbine on it.

"Almost as if we lived here," said Nancy.

The gingerbread was in a round pan.

"It's much easier," said Aunt Martha, "to cut a pie-shaped gingerbread into four equal pieces than into three, so it's lucky you came, Ben."

As they ate, Ben told about the city. About the trains that run under the ground, and the parades and band concerts; about the hurdy-gurdies, and the pushcarts where flowers and vegetables are sold. He told about the tall buildings and the ships in the harbor. And the people.

"There's about a million kids on my block," he said, "and there's always something going on. Day and night. You can go out at midnight, even, and there are people. It's never quiet and lonesome the way it is here."

It was plain that he loved everything about the city.

"No wonder you miss it," said Elsa, "but you'll like it here when you get used to it. You wait and see. There's an awful lot of things going on around here, too, only they don't show so much."

"Oh, look!" said Nancy. "There's Sir Silver Tail again!"

"Sir Who?" asked Ben, as they turned to look at the little gray squirrel. "Oh, you mean Buster."

"Buster!" said Nancy. "His name isn't Buster."

"How do you know?" asked Ben. "That's what I call him, anyway. Hi, Buster!"

"Have you tried to feed him?" asked Aunt Martha.

"Yes," said Ben, "but he's not very tame. He'll almost come, but not quite. I think he will when he gets to know me a little better."

"Well, he's one interesting thing about the country," said Elsa.

*111*

"Him!" said Ben. "Oh, he's all right; but you don't have to come to the country to see squirrels. There's millions of them in the parks. And pigeons, too."

There seemed to be nothing they could say to make Ben think he might someday like the country.

"I'm going back to the city as soon as I can earn the money," he said.

"But first you must come to the farm someday if you'd like to," said Aunt Martha. "Shall I go ask Mrs. Taylor if she'd be willing?"

"She's not home this afternoon; she's gone to see somebody that's sick," said Ben.

"We'll arrange it some other time then, and soon," said Aunt Martha. "And now, girls, we really must go. Thank you for your help, Ben."

"I'll look for you at school," said Elsa.

"And please ask Mr. Taylor to tell you all he can about the little house," said Nancy. "Who used to live in it, and if they had any children, and where they are now, and everything."

"Could you be a spy, do you think," asked Elsa, "and pretend you have to find out everything that's going on around here?"

"In the city I could be a detective," said Ben,

"but I can't see that there'd be anything to find out in the country."

"Well, *try!*" said Elsa.

"All right," said Ben.

"What an *interesting* afternoon!" said Elsa, as they drove away.

## Chapter 7

THURSDAY was Uncle Sven's day to go to town shopping.

"It may take me a little longer than usual to-day," he said to Aunt Martha, as he started out. "Whoa Emma needs new shoes."

The children were watching for him when he came back, and hurried out to help him carry the groceries into the house and to hear the news from Grandpa's store.

"Wait until I put Whoa Emma in the barn," he said, "and then I'll come in and tell you. I met a friend of yours."

"Who?" asked Elsa.

"You wait and I'll tell you the whole story," said Uncle Sven. "How about a cup of coffee, Martha?"

"I'll get it ready right away," said Aunt Martha.

While Uncle Sven sat drinking his coffee, he told about his adventure.

"When you told me Mr. Taylor took care of people's gardens," he said, "I wondered if he might be the man I've seen a few times in the store. I've seen him working in some of the gardens in town, too. So today I asked Grandpa, and he said a man named Taylor does come in now and then to buy Swedish bread; but he didn't know whether it was the one Ben lives with or not. He's very pleasant, Grandpa said, but he never has much to say—he's not the sociable kind, evidently. Well, I had my errands done and Whoa Emma was still at the blacksmith shop. It wasn't busy in the store so I thought I might as well sit and visit with Grandpa until Whoa Emma's shoes were ready. While we were talking, Mr. Taylor walked in."

"Oh, my goodness!" said Elsa. "Did you ask him about Ben?"

"Did you ask him about the little house?" said Nancy.

"Wait a minute, wait a minute," said Uncle Sven. "I haven't told you half of it yet. Ben was with him. Mrs. Taylor got your letter yesterday, Martha. Since you said in it that you were the daughter of Mr. Benson who has the Swedish grocery store in town, everybody is now pretty well introduced to everybody else. The Taylors will be glad to have Ben come to play with the children."

He turned to the girls.

"I didn't get much chance to talk to Ben, though," he said, "because he didn't have eyes for anybody but Karl the Twelfth."

"For Karl the Twelfth!" said Aunt Martha in surprise. "But he didn't pay the least bit of attention to Whoa Emma on Monday. I thought it rather strange at the time, because children are usually attracted to horses."

"Well, he paid attention to Karl the Twelfth, all right," said Uncle Sven. "He did come into the store for a minute after the baker brought the fresh bread and Grandpa called him in and gave him a coffee roll. But he asked if he could take it out and sit in the grocery wagon while he ate it. Of course Grandpa said he could and gave him some sugar for Karl the Twelfth; and off he went and that was the last I saw of him until I went out to go home.

"Mr. Taylor said they're pretty worried about Ben because he's so lonesome for the city. When they heard about Ben's being left without a home, Mr. Taylor thought it would be a good thing to take him. His wife isn't well and Ben could help about the house; and Mr. Taylor is beginning to be troubled with rheumatism and needs Ben's help, too. But it isn't working out very well. Ben seems to try to do what they ask him to, but his heart isn't in it. Mr. Taylor said he hadn't seen him show any real interest in anything before he took such a liking to Karl the Twelfth today."

"That *is* strange," said Aunt Martha, "that he took such a liking to Karl the Twelfth, I mean, when Whoa Emma didn't interest him at all. It's not strange that he's lonesome; that seems natural enough."

"Yes," said Uncle Sven. "Evidently the Taylors are trying their best to be kind to him, but I don't suppose living with them is very exciting for a child, and he's probably used to excitement."

"Yes, he is," said Elsa. "He told us how exciting it is in the city."

"He said a queer thing when I went to speak

to him as I was leaving," said Uncle Sven. "He was sitting in the wagon looking as sober as a judge, but when I said, 'So you think Karl the Twelfth is a pretty good old horse, do you?' he smiled a little and answered, 'Yes, he makes me think of the city.'"

"Makes him think of the city!" said Nancy in astonishment.

They couldn't help laughing to think of gentle, slow old Karl the Twelfth reminding anybody of the city with its trains running underground and overhead, and its thousands of people rushing around.

"That's what he said," said Uncle Sven. "I'm sure I can't make out what he meant."

"I think I can guess," said Aunt Martha. "It just came to me that it probably isn't Karl the Twelfth he's interested in so much as his grocery wagon. Ben is no doubt used to delivery wagons in the city. Whoa Emma was harnessed to a buggy, so she probably looked like a country horse to him; and Karl the Twelfth with his grocery wagon looked like a city horse."

"I never thought of that," said Uncle Sven. "I expect you're right."

The front doorbell rang. Of course it was Cuckoo Clock. Elsa ran to let her in.

"She'll be as famous for ringing the doorbell as Teddy is for drinking coffee," said Uncle Sven.

Then he set down his coffee cup, took out his pipe, and said, as casually as if he had been talking about the weather, "If you'd like to, girls, maybe tomorrow morning you can get a look at the inside of the little house."

"What!" said Elsa, jumping up so quickly that she knocked over her chair.

Nancy didn't even seem to notice the clatter.

"Do you really mean it, Uncle Sven?" she asked. "You aren't just teasing us?"

"I mean it," he answered. "Mr. Taylor says that every now and then he unboards the doors of the little house and gives it a good airing out. He plans to do so tomorrow morning if it's a nice day, as it's the only free morning he'll have for some time. If you and the girls care to go over, Martha, he'll show you the house. He says he's sure nobody will mind."

"We'll walk on tiptoe, Uncle Sven!" said Nancy. "And we won't touch anything. *What* if you hadn't gone to Grandpa's store today!"

"Don't forget," said Uncle Sven, "that Mr. Taylor said he'd air the house only if it's a nice day. If it's damp and rainy, he doesn't want to open it. But I don't think you need to worry; I'm pretty sure it's going to be fair tomorrow."

"All we can do is hope," said Aunt Martha. "I do believe I'm getting as much interested in that little house as you are, girls. It *will* be fun to go inside, won't it?"

As soon as Nancy and Elsa woke up Friday morning, they thought of the weather. The sky was clear and blue. They could go to the little silver house!

Right after breakfast they set out. Mr. Taylor and Ben were waiting for them. Both the back and front doors of the house were open but the windows were still boarded up.

"I have brought a lantern," said Mr. Taylor, "because we'll not get enough light from the doorways. If you'll excuse me for going in front of you, I'll step in to lead the way."

Aunt Martha and the children followed him through the front door into a little hall. There was a door on each side and Mr. Taylor led them into the room on the right.

"This must be the sitting room," said Aunt Martha.

The children said nothing; it felt so strange to be inside a boarded-up house! The open front doorway gave only part of the room a little light; the rest of it was dark. Mr. Taylor lit his lantern and, as he carried it around the room, it made strange shadows dance on the walls. By its light they could see that the room had a fireplace but that, too, was boarded up.

Nancy thought the little house looked even more lonesome inside than it did outside.

They went into the room on the other side of the hall, and then into the kitchen.

Ben followed them but he didn't seem interested in any part of the house. Aunt Martha, on the other hand, was asking Mr. Taylor all kinds of questions, and seemed pleased at his answers. She seemed particularly interested to see how well built the little house was, and how carefully it had been kept in repair. She remarked that the chimneys were probably still all right; and that, though the wallpaper was faded, it was whole in most places. She said that, since the house was so well built, it wouldn't be hard to heat. She even seemed glad to hear that the cellar was warm and dry.

Nancy and Elsa were not interested in this conversation. They only wanted to know who had lived in the little house and why it had stood empty so long.

They all went into the front hall again and up the narrow stairway.

At the back of the house upstairs there was an unfinished attic just as there was at Aunt Martha's. At the front there were two small bedrooms with sloping ceilings and tiny windows.

Mr. Taylor, Aunt Martha, and Ben walked back into the attic, but Nancy and Elsa lingered in the bedroom that was directly over the sitting room.

"The maple tree must be outside that window," said Elsa. "If children slept in this room, they could get out of the window and climb down the tree in the night and have an adventure, and I bet they did, too."

"And in the daytime they maybe got into the tree and sat and read," said Nancy.

"Or built a kind of tree house," said Elsa.

But they forgot the tree the next moment, for Aunt Martha called, "Mr. Taylor has something to show you, girls."

They hurried into the attic. Mr. Taylor was lifting a big package up into his arms. It was wrapped in newspapers.

"There was no paper around it when I found it," he said. "It was standing in that corner, leaning against the wall. You will see that the back of it is about the same color as the attic boards; so it may be that nobody noticed it when the rest

*123*

of the things were moved out of the house. We'll take it outdoors so you can see it better."

Aunt Martha took the lantern and led the way downstairs.

"It looks like a great big picture," said Nancy.

It was a picture. When Mr. Taylor had taken it out of its wrappings, he held it so they could all see it.

"O-o-o-h," said Nancy and Elsa.

"What a lovely child!" said Aunt Martha.

It was a picture of a little girl about three or four years old. She had brown eyes and golden-brown curly hair, parted in the middle. She wore an old-fashioned dress of an orange-gold color with brown stripes. She had a small brown velvet bag in her hand. She looked like a happy child although she was not smiling. Having her portrait painted must have been a serious matter—too serious for smiling.

"She's beautiful," said Nancy.

"She looks alive," said Elsa.

"It doesn't look like a picture in a house," said Ben. "It looks like one in an art museum."

It seemed that Ben knew about art museums as well as about hurdy-gurdies and pushcarts, and trains that ran under the ground.

Mr. Taylor smiled at him. "That's what I

thought," he said. "I thought it might be valuable and I didn't like to take the responsibility for it; so I told the lawyer about it. He said he didn't know much about pictures himself, but he had a friend who did and who was coming to visit him that next week. They drove out here one day. His friend looked at the picture and I could see that he was interested in it, but he said it wasn't valuable as far as money goes. He thinks it was probably done by one of the traveling artists who used to go from town to town and earn their living by painting portraits such as this."

Mr. Taylor let the children look at every part of the picture and the frame, but they could not find any name anywhere. There was nothing to show who the little girl was. She was an unusually lovely child. That was all anybody could say.

It was enough to keep Nancy and Elsa talking about her all the way back to the farm, and most of the afternoon and evening. It seemed wonderful to them that such a beautiful little girl should in some way be connected with the little silver house. But it seemed all wrong that her picture should be left there in the darkness.

"Something *has* to be done about it," said Elsa decidedly.

But neither she nor Nancy could think of anything they could do.

This was their last evening at the farm. On Saturday afternoon Aunt Martha and Uncle Sven drove them home. The other travelers had already returned and they all met for supper at Grandma's, so they could have one more visit with Uncle George and Aunt Hanna before they left for Chicago on the eight o'clock train.

Everyone—grownups and children—went to the station with them. It was sad to think of their going, but their coming had brought much happiness for all to remember.

"I thought the spring was wonderful," Nancy told Aunt Hanna, "but the topsy-turvy weeks have been just as good."

"And you have something even better ahead of you," answered Aunt Hanna.

"What?" asked Nancy.

"Your first Long Swedish Christmas," said Aunt Hanna. "And I don't know of any place where Christmas is as lovely as it is at the Bensons'. You're a lucky little girl."

Although it was only October, the children were already beginning to talk about Christmas. While Mrs. Brown and Alex had been at his grandmother's, his uncle had also come to visit her. He had begun to teach Alex how to carve little figures out of wood. His mother was so pleased to see how clever he was with his hands that she decided to engage a teacher to give him more lessons in woodcarving. Alex was enjoying this work so much that he planned to make wooden Christmas gifts for all his friends.

Helga had had a wonderful time with her little cousins, Frank and Laura. Now she was waiting for Grandma to take her to call on John August. She was determined to make Christmas presents for all these babies. Her mother had cut out and basted three bibs for her. Helga planned to hem them with colored thread—pink for Laura and blue for Frank. For John August, the newest baby, she thought she would like to use two rows of stitches, one blue and the other pink.

"She's trying awfully hard," Sigrid told Nancy, "but you should see the stitches. They're a mile long and all crooked."

"One thing is sure anyway," said Elsa. "The babies won't care."

Sigrid was so enthusiastic about the girls' sewing club at Grandmother Carlson's and about the sale they were going to have that she wanted the Crimson Ramblers to have one, too.

"Then we'd really be *doing* something," she said. "If we got a sale ready for Thanksgiving time, we could use the money to pack Christmas boxes for poor children."

Nancy and Elsa had not thought much about Christmas.

"We've been thinking mostly about the little house," said Nancy.

"And about the picture of the little girl," said Elsa.

"I didn't see much use in trying to find out anything about a house that looked just like an ordinary house to me," said Alex, "but that picture makes it different. That's a real mystery. Mamma's got a history of this town, and I'm going to read it to see if it's got anything in it about the Crane family."

"I wish we could see the picture of that little girl, too," said Helga.

"So do I," said Sigrid. "Maybe someday Mr. Taylor will show it to us. But, anyway, we'll have to find out who she is, and some way to get her picture out of that dark house. I never heard of anything so foolish! To go and shut up a beautiful picture where nobody can see it! Old Jacob must have been even more ornery that Mr. Maple said he was."

"I still don't believe Old Jacob was ornery," said Elsa. "I *like* Old Jacob."

"You're ornery yourself," said Sigrid.

Even Ben showed an interest in the picture.

"I'm being a detective," he told Elsa at school one day.

"You are!" she said. "Good for you! I thought you didn't think there was anything to hunt for."

"I didn't," said Ben, "until Mr. Taylor showed us that little girl. Now I'm hunting every spare minute to find some clue to prove that she lived in the little house."

When Elsa reported this conversation to the Crimson Ramblers, they decided to ask Ben to become a member. Alex was delighted at the thought of having another boy in the club.

"First we have to ask Grandpa, though," said Nancy, "because all members should have a vote."

Grandpa thought it was a fine idea to ask Ben to join the club.

"It will be fun for you to have him," he said, "and perhaps it will help Ben a little in his loneliness. Karl the Twelfth, Oscar, and I all vote yes."

Grandpa agreed with Sigrid that a club like the Crimson Ramblers ought to be doing something to help somebody.

"Like having a sale?" asked Sigrid hopefully.

"No," said Grandpa, "I think having a sale is more for a club that's connected with a church or school. I think it would be better if you did something yourselves instead of asking people to buy things from you. Why don't you make this a Crimson Rambler Christmas?"

"What's that?" asked Nancy.

"It's something that came into my head this minute," said Grandpa. "And I think's it's something you could do. I'll give you one idea: Grandma has been saying how sorry she feels for Ben's grandmother because she must be both lonesome for him and worried about him. Why don't you help Ben pack a Christmas box for her? You can think of all sorts of little surprises to put in. And I'm sure you'll have lots of other ideas for things you could do to make a Crimson Rambler Christmas."

A Crimson Rambler Christmas appealed to all the members.

"At last we'll be *doing* something," said Sigrid.

"It will be something *different*," said Elsa.

Soon after Ben became a Crimson Rambler, the club changed its meeting day. Because Grandpa had seen how much Ben loved Karl the Twelfth and his grocery wagon, he had asked Mr. Taylor if Ben could help deliver groceries Saturday afternoons during November and December. That was a very busy time for Grandpa. Not only the Swedish people in town, but many others, too, wanted to buy the good Christmas things he imported from Sweden.

"I don't want to say anything to Ben unless it seems perfectly all right to you," Grandpa told Mr. Taylor, "because I know you need him."

Mr. Taylor said he thought the important thing right now was to try to get Ben over his loneliness. Working on the grocery wagon might help, and he would be glad to have Ben do it.

This plan seemed to be the one thing in Ben's new life that made him happy, and nothing would have induced him to give it up. So now the Ramblers met on Thursday after school.

Every evening at supper Nancy had interesting things to tell Grandma and Grandpa about school, or club meetings, or Christmas plans.

"Ben and Alex are getting to be good friends," she said one night. "I think Ben likes Alex best of all of us; but he told me he feels so bad because Alex can't walk. He said in a way Alex is lucky because he has so many nice things, and his mother is so good to him. Ben says there's a boy named Dick on his block in the city. Dick can't walk either and he doesn't even have a wheel chair. He has hardly any nice things, and nobody to pay much attention to him, because his mother has to be out working all day. I think Dick must have been one of Ben's best friends. I think he worries about Dick."

A few evenings later Nancy reported:

"The Crimson Ramblers are going to send a Christmas box to Ben's friend Dick. Alex suggested it and Ben is so glad. We're going to make it the best of all our Christmas surprises."

"Good!" said Grandpa. "That's great."


And so autumn went by, and the children were busy and happy. Although school and club meetings filled most of the time, there were extra pleasures, too.

There was Halloween when Alex and his mother gave a party. The children bobbed for apples, popped corn, and played the games Mrs. Brown had invented to fit the occasion.

Elsa had a name day in October, and Helga had one in November. They celebrated them at Grandma's with name-day cakes and crowns, and all the festivity a proper name-day celebration should have.

Thanksgiving came, and the Bensons and Carlsons had a wonderful day at the farm. In the evening the girls walked down to the little schoolhouse at the foot of the hill to see the Thanksgiving play for which Wanda had been practicing so long. This was the schoolhouse Nancy had helped to decorate with daisies and buttercups in the springtime. She looked at the Thanksgiving decorations with interest. The schoolchildren had arranged evergreen branches and copper-colored oak leaves over the windows and doors. At the front of the platform were more green branches and copper-colored leaves; and nestling among them were great golden pumpkins and squashes. The decorations were pretty, and exactly right for Thanksgiving; but Nancy liked the daisies and buttercups better.

The play was about a little girl who fell asleep and dreamed she was present at the First Thanksgiving. Wanda was that little girl, and she had a longer part than anybody else in the play. Sigrid, Nancy, Elsa, and Helga were all proud of her.

"That was a good ending for a Thanksgiving day," said Elsa, as they were on their way home.

"And now," said Sigrid, "only two more days, and then Christmas begins."

"Of all the times of all the year," said Elsa, "Christmas is the best."

## Chapter 8

THE Long Swedish Christmas begins on the first Sunday in Advent.

"Just what *is* Advent?" asked Nancy one evening, as she and Grandma and Grandpa sat talking about Christmas plans.

"It is the time of preparation for the coming of the Christ Child," said Grandpa, "the time to get our homes and our gifts ready for Christmas. And, most of all, the time to think about what Christmas really means and why we celebrate it."

"The four Sundays before Christmas are called

the Advent Sundays," said Grandma. "Perhaps the girls have told you that they always come to us those Sundays for the lighting of the Advent candles."

"Yes," said Nancy, "and to hear the stories and the Christmas songs. Elsa told me. She says it's *beautiful*."

Grandma smiled. "We'll have our own family here as usual this year, of course," she said. "And invite Alex and his mother, and Ben, too. And I thought that, since there are four Sundays, you four girls might like to take one each and choose one person you'd like to have as your special guest that day."

"Oh, won't that be fun?" said Nancy, and went to bed thinking about it. When the Carlson girls came up after school the next day, they were as happy as she had been to hear about Grandma's plan.

"I know," said Helga, "I know right off the person I want. John August."

"But that would be more than one person," said Sigrid. "He couldn't come all by himself."

"Oh, dear," said Helga. "It seems as if a baby ought to be invited. The little Christ Child was a baby."

"Helga is right," said Grandma, "and for John

August we'll make an exception. We'll invite his mother and father, too."

"Thank you, thank you, Grandma," said Helga, running to hug her. "Which Sunday can he come?"

"We'll wait until you've all chosen," said Grandma. "We'll have to see which Sunday is most convenient for each of the guests."

"I could ask some girl in my room at school or in my Sunday school class," said Sigrid, "but the trouble is, if I ask Clara, then Grace will think it's funny I didn't ask her; and if I ask Sophie, Mary will wonder why I didn't choose her."

Elsa was having the same kind of trouble, but suddenly she had an idea.

"I know," she said. "I'd like to ask Mr. Sanborn. I'm sure he's the person I choose."

Mr. Sanborn lived next door to the Carlsons. He had hundreds of books in his house and sometimes he let Elsa come into his bookroom to read. There were no children's books there, but she found a great deal to interest her, anyway. Mr. Sanborn said she was a real "bookworm."

"Do you think Mr. Sanborn would want to come?" asked Grandma.

"Oh, yes," said Elsa decidedly. "He'd love to."

Grandma looked doubtful but she said that Elsa might invite him.

"If he doesn't care to come, you can ask someone else," she said.

"He'll want to, all right," said Elsa.

Now Sigrid had thought of someone.

"Wanda!" she said. "She could ride with Uncle Sven and Aunt Martha when they come."

All the girls were pleased to think Wanda was to be invited. Now only Nancy was left to make a choice.

"Can't you decide?" asked Sigrid.

"Oh, yes, I've decided," said Nancy, "but I don't know if we could do it."

"What is it?" asked Grandma. "Tell us."

"I'd like to have an animal," said Nancy. "Animals came to the first Christmas."

"An animal!" said Sigrid.

"Not a cow, I hope!" said Elsa.

"No," said Nancy, "a dog. I'd like to have Danny."

"Well, we'll have to think about that a little," said Grandma. "Of course Danny would be welcome. But he is really needed at the farm, especially when his family go away."

"That's just it," said Nancy. "That's partly

why I want to ask him. Because he always has to stay at home. Oscar can go on rides and visiting, but never Danny."

Grandma smiled. "I'm not sure he'd care to, and besides what would Teddy do? Danny is a strange dog to him; Teddy might be scared, or at any rate feel that Danny shouldn't be here."

But now all the girls were thrilled at having an animal guest at the Advent candle burning.

"Danny is so good, Grandma," said Sigrid. "Teddy couldn't be afraid of him."

"And he's never, never been away in all his life," said Helga.

"And animals all love each other at Christmas," said Elsa. "Teddy and Danny would lie down together like the lion and the lamb."

"You are little monkeys, all four of you," said Grandma. "We'll see. We can't decide about Danny until we talk to Uncle Sven."

And she did talk to him, the next time he came to town.

"What those children don't think of!" said Uncle Sven, laughing. "I never thought I'd have to make plans for Danny to go out visiting. Let me think about it and we'll see what can be done."

And that was how it happened that matters were arranged so that Danny could be Nancy's guest on the first Sunday of Advent. Fred, who had cooked such good bacon for the sunrise breakfast in September, promised to bring his own dog to the farm that Sunday, and to take care of everything until Danny came home.

Mrs. Brown invited Ben to stay overnight with Alex after each Advent candle lighting, so that he wouldn't have to walk home alone in the darkness.

It was, of course, much too early to put up the Christmas tree, but on Saturday Uncle Sven brought in some evergreen branches which Grandma and Nancy arranged in the sitting room. Grandma set her four-branched candleholder on a table near the wall, and put four white candles in it.

"We will burn one candle each Sunday," she said, "and when the fourth candle is burned down to the end, then it will be Christmas."

Grandma made both rye bread and white coffee bread on Saturday. This, with cold meat and cheese, coffee and cocoa, would be their Sunday night supper.

The children made little Christmas decorations from spruce twigs and red ribbon for the dogs to wear on their collars; and a red necktie for Teddy.

"Be sure to tie Teddy's loosely," said Grandma,

"so that if he gets excited it will come off at once, and not hurt him."

"I'll watch him," said Nancy, "and if his necktie bothers him, I'll take it right off. We want everybody to be happy at Christmas."

The candle was to be lighted at four o'clock. A little before that time, Nancy and Grandpa got Oscar and Teddy ready.

"See that you behave yourself, young man!" said Grandpa, picking Teddy up. "If you don't, out to the barn you go!"

Teddy stuck out his tongue and gave Grandpa's nose a quick lick.

"See," said Nancy, "he's saying, 'You wouldn't send me out to the barn. I know you wouldn't.'"

Uncle Sven, Aunt Martha, and Danny were the last to arrive; and it was not Teddy who caused the trouble. It was Oscar. He had stood up on his hind legs to look out of the dining room window when he heard Whoa Emma's wagon coming. When he saw his friend, Danny, he was so happy that he was almost frantic. He came rushing through the kitchen like a small whirlwind and knocked over Helga and one of Grandma's flowering plants.

Helga was not hurt. After her first surprise, she got up laughing. But Grandma's plant pot was broken and the best blossoms were knocked off the plant. In all the excitement, nobody thought to look at Teddy until Nancy suddenly remembered that she had promised to watch him. He was sitting in a corner of the kitchen with his eyes blazing and his tail twice its natural size. When Nancy came close to him, she could hear him making little growling noises.

"It's all right, Teddy," she said. "Danny won't hurt you."

"Come, Teddy," said Uncle Sven, with one hand on Danny's collar and the other held out toward Teddy, while Grandpa held Oscar to try to quiet him a little.

But now it seemed that Teddy was not in the least afraid of Danny, nor was he intending to attack him. Teddy was interested only in Oscar. He and Oscar had been brought up together since their kitten and puppy days. When they were tiny, they had often slept together in the same basket. As they grew older, Oscar still wanted to be near Teddy, but Teddy had not wanted to bother with a lively dog, and seldom paid any attention to his friend. Now, however, another animal had appeared and Oscar was making the greatest possible fuss about him.

"Whose dog is Oscar, anyway?" Teddy seemed

to be thinking. At any rate, he did not go to Uncle Sven, but straight to Oscar. He got as close to him as possible.

"Well, for goodness' sake!" said Grandma. "I do believe Teddy is jealous."

All evening Teddy, who usually paid so little attention to Oscar, wanted to be near his old friend.

When all the people had gone into the sitting room, Uncle Sven called Danny to come and lie down beside his chair. Danny obeyed instantly. Oscar followed and lay down as close to Danny as he could get. Along came Teddy and settled himself beside Oscar. When Danny moved a little nearer to Uncle Sven, Oscar moved nearer to Danny, and Teddy snuggled more tightly against Oscar.

"Poor Oscar," said Aunt Martha, "you'll be squeezed into a sausage between the two of them."

Oscar didn't mind; he looked completely happy.

"It's just the way Elsa said," Helga kept telling everybody. "All animals are friends at Christmas-time."

As Grandma got up to light the first candle, Grandpa read from the Bible the verses with which they always opened their Christmas celebration. He began, " 'The night is far spent; the day is at hand: let us therefore cast off the works of darkness, and let us put on the armour of light.' "

The children did not understand fully the meaning of all the words he read, and he did not try to explain everything to them. When he had finished reading, he said only, "Although the light of the candles is an important part of Christmas now, and on Lucia Day, and at Christmastime itself, it is not the candles that are the real 'armour of light.' It is, instead, the love and kindness we shall try to show in all this Christmas season, so that we shall have, in everything we do, the real spirit of Christmas."

Then he turned to Uncle John.

"Shall we sing now?" he said, and Uncle John began to sing an old Swedish Christmas carol.

Nancy watched the candle—the only light in the room—as they sat there singing one lovely carol after another. Sometimes they stopped singing and talked about Christmas instead.

After a while Grandma got up. "We will get supper now," she said.

They went into the dining room, but the candle still burned on.

"When it is all burned down," Helga told Alex and Ben, "then there will be only three more Sundays until Christmas."

The animals got up, too. Danny began to feel at home in his new surroundings and wandered around the house. Oscar, of course, was right beside him, and Teddy beside Oscar.

When Uncle Sven took the dogs for a little walk after supper, Teddy, who usually couldn't be persuaded to go out on a cold night, had to go, too. Grandpa and the children watched them from the window. Danny walked on one side of Uncle Sven and Teddy on the other. Oscar ran round and round them barking his happiest bark.

"They are such good friends at Christmas," said Helga.

When the good friends came in again, everybody gathered once more in the sitting room. The candle was only two inches high now.

"Candle," said Elsa, "please don't burn too fast. We want to stay a long time."

Grandma read the Christmas story from the Bible. The Carlson girls always asked for this every Advent Sunday.

"'And there were in the same country shepherds abiding in the field, keeping watch over their flocks by night. And, lo, the angel of the Lord came upon them, and the glory of the Lord shone round about them. . . .' "

After the story, they neither sang nor talked. They sat quietly for a while, watching the candle. Then Uncle John began to sing again and the others listened until the candle began to sputter and crackle, and the flame went out.

"Only three more Sundays to Christmas!" said Helga, jumping up.

"Shh—shh," said her mother softly; and Grandpa, pulling Helga close to his knee, added gently, "And may the glory of the Lord shine upon us all to help us keep this Christmas season."

And now began a very busy time. There was all the regular work for the grownups, and school for the children, but every spare minute was used for Christmas preparation.

The Crimson Ramblers were getting a box ready for Nancy's mother in the hospital, and one for Ben's grandmother. Most important of all was the box they were going to pack for Ben's friend, Dick.

"I wish we could send him a wheel chair," said Alex.

But a wheel chair cost far too much.

"He will be glad of other things, though," said Ben. "He will be glad to have packages to open. It would be fun if he could have more packages to open than any other kid on the block."

"Will some of them have many?" asked Elsa.

"No, not many," said Ben, "but a few may have three or four."

"Then Dick should have a dozen," said Elsa.

"Does he like to read?" asked Alex.

"Yes," said Ben. "I used to let him take my library books."

"Then I will send him one of my books," said Alex.

"We should each send him something of our own," said Sigrid.

"What?" asked Helga.

"We should send him something we want ourselves; not just something we don't want any more," said Sigrid decidedly.

"If we each bought or made him something, and then gave him some special thing of our own," said Elsa, "that would make one dozen presents."

Mrs. Brown said she would pay for sending the box to Dick when it was ready.

"One thing I wish," said Nancy, "is that we could think of some present to give the little house."

The other girls agreed that this was a wonderful idea.

"But what could it be?" asked Helga.

"What could you give a house nobody lives in?" asked Sigrid.

"We could make a Christmas wreath to hang on the front door," said Helga.

"Somehow, to have a wreath on the door and nothing inside just seems to make the house more lonesome," said Elsa.

"Well, let's keep thinking," said Sigrid. "Maybe something will come to us."

There was so much to think about and so much to do that the first week of Christmas was far too short.

"We'll have to hurry faster than this," said Sigrid, "or we'll never be ready."


To Elsa's delight, Mr. Sanborn said he would be happy to come to the burning of the second Advent candle. His coming made that Sunday one of the happiest of all—for the grownups and the children.

He had traveled a great deal and had even been to Bethlehem. He had seen the very place where the little Christ Child was born. He had seen the fields where the shepherds watched their flocks, and the road along which the Three Wise Men had come to bring their gifts. He told about it while the Advent candle was burning. Sitting there as the room grew darker and the candle shone more brightly, the children were thrilled with his story. To Grandpa and Grandma, it seemed one of the loveliest things that happened all that Christmas season.

While supper was being prepared, the children gathered around Mr. Sanborn. Although he was Elsa's friend, she seldom had a good chance to talk to him, for she had promised her mother she would never disturb him when he let her come into his bookroom to read. Now she wanted to tell him all about the little silver house and to ask his advice. She had great faith that Mr. Sanborn knew practically everything.

He listened with interest to all she had to say. When she had finished, he said he had heard about the Cranes. But he didn't know that Old Jacob had made a will which prevented the family from selling the house or even from renting it. "It's not the first time, though," he added, "that property has been tied up by some foolish will."

Elsa told him, too, about the picture Mr. Taylor had found.

"We do want to know what the little girl's

name is," she said. "Can you think of any way to find out?"

Mr. Sanborn said he didn't know whether or not he could find out anything about the house or about the picture, but he would do his best, and if he did learn anything, he would let them know at once.

"We'd like to give the little house a Christmas present," said Nancy. "It looks so lonesome."

"But what in the world would you give a lonesome house that nobody lives in?" asked Sigrid.

"Well now, that *is* a question," said Mr. Sanborn.

And just then Grandma called them to supper.

After supper Grandma told about some of the things she had done as a child in Sweden at Christmastime. About the Lucia custom and the Long Dance of Christmas Eve and the early morning service in the church on Christmas Day.

"And, of course," she went on, "we always remembered the animals, too, at Christmas, with extra oats or a bone, or whatever they liked best to eat. And we always put out sheaves of grain for the birds."

"There!" said Mr. Sanborn. "There's the answer to your question about what to give the little house, children. You could put out grain for the birds and they would come and be near the house and it would not be all alone at Christmas."

"That is the most wonderful idea anybody has had yet," said Sigrid.

The other children agreed.

"But when can we do it?" asked Alex.

That was a problem. If only the little house weren't so far away!

"You'd need to begin right off," said Grandma, "so that by Christmas the birds would have discovered the grain and be used to coming to the house."

"Maybe," said Aunt Martha, "if all you children helped provide the food, Ben would take care of the feeding."

"Oh, would you, Ben?" asked Alex. "We'll use some of our Christmas money to buy grain. And maybe we can save crumbs, too."

"We will!" said Elsa. "And we'll plan our Christmas money all over again, to take in the birds."

"Will you do it, Ben?" asked Nancy.

"All right," said Ben.

"And tell us if the birds come," said Sigrid.

"It surely is lucky you came, Mr. Sanborn," said Elsa.

Now the candle would not burn much longer,

so it was time for the Christmas story. Uncle Sven read it this time, and it was in the minds of all who listened that their guest had really been in the country where all this happened.

After the story, they sang *O Little Town of Bethlehem;* and once again an Advent candle went out. Now there were only two left in Grandma's lovely Swedish candleholder.

*Chapter* 9

Of all the children, it was Nancy who thought about the little house most. No matter how busy she was with Christmas plans and work, pictures of the little house would come flashing into her mind.

She would see it as it had looked the night they first rode out to it—silver in the moonlight. Or imagine how it would look in the springtime when the garden was coming back to life and the flowers they had planted for Traveler's Joy were blossoming by the roadside.

She pictured it, too, on dark nights without the moonlight; and on the cold gray mornings when there was no sun to warm it. She wished she could see it with the birds around it. She did not know what birds would come to a little country house in winter. But Grandpa and Karl the Twelfth were so busy now that they had no time for rambling.

Then Mrs. Brown had a good idea. She put a small feeding station in her back yard, so that the two pupils in her school could watch the birds. Chickadees and juncos came, along with the sparrows and the beautiful but saucy bluejays. There was even a downy woodpecker with a bright red spot on his head. Now, when Nancy came home for dinner at noon, she always had something to tell Grandma and Grandpa about the birds. And now she could picture the birds at the little house.

Ben didn't have a chance to see the birds much himself. But Mrs. Taylor walked over to watch them a little while every day, and sent word to the children that the little house now had a great deal of company.

Mr. Sanborn kept his promise to try to find out something about the house and the picture of the little girl. One day after school the Carlson girls came hurrying to tell Nancy and Alex what Mr. Sanborn had learned.

"Mr. Sanborn says he didn't really find out anything about the picture," Elsa reported. "But he did find out that Old Jacob built the little house when he was a young man, and his three sons and one little daughter were born in it. And the little daughter's name was Mariette. And, what do you think! She died when she was only ten, and I think the picture is of her. Mr. Sanborn said it was an unusual name for a little New England girl. Marietta is common, but not Mariette. I think it's beautiful."

"She died when she was only ten!" said Nancy solemnly. "When she was only a little girl!"

"Yes," said Elsa. "At first I thought it was so sad. I couldn't go to sleep last night and I got up and went out in the kitchen and told Mamma. And she said we mustn't feel sad. We must remember the song we love to have Grandpa sing to us, about nobody is safer than God's little children. And Mamma said we must remember that God keeps his little children just as safe whether they're living in this world or have died into the next. And now I'm glad she died when she was ten!"

"Glad!" said Nancy.

"Well, maybe I ought not to be," said Elsa. "But if she was only ten when she died, it seems as if she is still ten and as if, in a way, she still lives in the little silver house—not a grown-up lady but a little girl."

"But we haven't got anything to prove that the picture is Mariette," said Alex.

"Oh, it is!" said Nancy. "You'd know it is, if only you could see it. It *must* be."

Sigrid asked Grandpa if they could ask Mr. Taylor to unwrap the picture again so they could all see it.

"Sometime after Christmas," said Grandpa. "Everybody is too busy just now."

The Crimson Ramblers thought they were busiest of all. When they told Grandma they had decided that they would each buy or make one thing for Dick and give him one thing of their own—something they really loved themselves—she smiled at them.

"Now you are showing that you are real Christmas children," she said. "To give gladly something you want yourself—that is the real spirit of Christmas."

But when it came to deciding definitely to part with something, they all found it harder than they had thought it would be.

Sigrid made up her mind at once and stuck to her decision as she usually did. She would send Dick the box of crayons Grandma Carlson had given her. Sigrid loved to draw and these crayons were much nicer than any she had ever had before. When the other children tried to tell her how good they thought she was, she didn't seem to want to talk about it.

"I think she's afraid she'll cry," said Elsa. "She loves those crayons."

Elsa's dearest possessions were the few books she owned. Her favorite was a book of fairy tales and legends. In it were stories of the Sleeping Beauty, and Snow White and Rose Red; of the Ugly Duckling, and the Little Mermaid; of Aladdin, and Ali Baba; and of Jason and the Golden Fleece. There were twenty-five stories and Elsa loved them all. Should she send this book to Dick? No, he would like *Swiss Family Robinson* just as well. That is what she had decided before Grandma called the Crimson Ramblers "real Christmas children."

Elsa went home and put *Swiss Family Robinson* back in the bookcase. Even a boy couldn't possibly like it so well as Aladdin and Ali Baba, and Jason and the Golden Fleece. She took out *Fairy Tales and Legends* for Dick. It was hard to give it up, though; and nobody but Elsa would ever know how many times the two books changed places before Dick's box was packed.

Alex decided to send Dick a favorite book, too: his *Robinson Crusoe*. Helga planned to send her dominoes. Nancy didn't know what to send. Her books had been left at home when she came to visit Grandma. Surely Dick would not want a doll, even if she could have brought herself to part with Charlotte. Neither would he want her chain and locket, or her Swedish costume, or her Alice in Wonderland apron.

Then she thought of the riddle book. The book with one hundred and one riddles that Papa had sent her in the spring and that had given so much pleasure to them all. She almost wished she hadn't thought of it until it was too late! Then she remembered what Grandma had said about real Christmas children.

"Would Dick like my riddle book?" she asked Ben.

"Oh, *yes!*" said Ben, with so much enthusiasm that Nancy knew she would have to part with it. "He can ask all the kids riddles. It will be great."

Ben had so few things of his own that the other children wondered how he could find anything to put in Dick's box. He told them rather gruffly, "I'm going to send Dick a quarter. My grandmother gave it to me just before she went to the Home. She said it was for an emergency."

"A whole quarter!" said Sigrid. "I bet Dick never had a quarter in his life. That's *wonderful!*"

Ben turned red, but he looked pleased. He showed the children how Mrs. Taylor had polished the quarter for him with silver polish so that it looked bright and new. She had found a small cardboard box with cotton in it for the quarter to lie on. It looked like a very special kind of present.

Nancy bought some paper to go with Sigrid's crayons; and Helga used two of her pennies for a pencil with an eraser on it. Sigrid made some molasses cookies all herself, and Ben gathered and shelled some nuts. Elsa took some post cards and carefully cut each one into pieces to make a picture puzzle.

The children thought Alex had the best present of all for Dick. When the Crimson Rambler Club was formed, Mrs. Brown had thoughtfully taken a picture of the members to send to Nancy's mother. Now she took another picture with Ben in it, too. Alex made three frames from thin wood, so that Ben's grandmother, Nancy's mother, and

Dick could each hang a copy of the little picture on the wall.

Ben was delighted with this.

"Now they can see how Karl the Twelfth and his wagon look," he said.

While they were wrapping the presents and packing the box, Ben talked more than he had at any time since the children had known him. He made Dick, lying alone by his window all day, seem so real that they all felt glad to be sending him some of their dearest possessions.

"Nancy!" said Elsa. "Remember those emergency stamps we saved when we were writing letters at the farm? We should use one for a Crimson Rambler letter to Dick. Then he will have a letter and a box, too."

Mrs. Brown brought them some paper, and each member of the club wrote a sentence or two in the letter.

"An emergency stamp is a good idea," said Nancy.

"I thought it would be," said Elsa.

On the third Sunday in Advent, Wanda was the guest. They sang Christmas songs when the candle first began to burn, but after a little while Grandma said that, since Wanda was with them, it would be a good time to begin to make their Christmas *karameller*.

"Oh, yes!" said Helga, jumping up at once. "It's *such* fun to make *karameller*."

Grandma and Nancy had already put on the dining room table many pieces of colored tissue paper, some gilt and silver paper, and some small colored pictures cut from magazines. Grandma, Aunt Anna, and Aunt Martha had been saving this kind of thing all year, because every Swedish house must have *karameller* for Christmas. There were scissors and paste on the table, too; and three plates of candy.

One plate held fudge—not the rich maple butternut fudge Aunt Martha made once or twice a year. That would be too expensive for *karameller*. This was plain brown-sugar fudge without any nuts. Each piece was about three inches long, an inch wide, and a quarter of an inch thick.

On another plate were peppermint sticks from Grandpa's store. They were about half an inch thick and Grandpa had cut them into pieces three inches long.

On the third plate were broken pieces of fudge and peppermint sticks for the children to eat.

Aunt Anna showed them how to wrap a *kara-mell*.

She cut a strip of light blue tissue paper six inches wide and long enough to wrap several times around a piece of fudge. She wrapped the fudge so that it came right in the middle of the paper, with an inch and a half of paper left over at each end. Then she pasted the paper down securely so the fudge would not slip out. At each end of the *karamell*, she cut the paper into strips to make fringe.

Then she wrapped a peppermint-stick *karamell* the same way.

She pasted a picture of a pink rose on the blue *karamell*. She cut a very narrow strip of gilt paper, and wound it around the pink peppermint-stick *karamell*.

"Of course you don't have to make them this way exactly," she said. "You'll all have some good ideas about ways to make them look pretty. But be sure to wrap the paper so that it is smooth and tight, and paste it on securely."

"And be sure to have fringe," said Helga.

"Oh, yes," said Aunt Anna. "They wouldn't be proper *karameller* without fringe."

Sigrid made a white *karamell*. Instead of using a picture from a magazine, she drew and colored some holly, and pasted that on the *karamell*. Nancy made a red one and decorated it with some pieces cut from a lace-paper doily. They looked like snowflakes. Wanda wrapped a *karamell* in two pieces of tissue paper—one pink, and one blue. The two colors made the fringe look very gay.

While the children were working, the men sat in the sitting room singing Swedish Christmas songs.

By suppertime there was a big plate full of *karameller* on the table. But there were not nearly enough to last until Christmas. The children would have to keep on making more; for, beginning tomorrow, Lucia Day, *karameller* would be offered to every guest who came to the house.

After supper Alex read the Christmas story, and the children sang carols. Ben chose the last one: "It Came Upon the Midnight Clear."

"Nancy, you'll *love* tomorrow," said Elsa, as the Carlsons were leaving.

"I know," said Helga, "tomorrow is Lucia Day."

About half-past five Monday morning, Nancy was wakened by the sound of Grandpa's voice singing a Swedish carol. She was wide awake in an instant and sat up in bed in the darkness. Teddy came dashing through the hall and bounded up onto the bed beside her. In a minute she could hear Grandpa and Grandma coming up the stairs. She could see that there was some kind of light coming through the hall.

Then Grandma stood in the doorway.

She was dressed in white. On her head was a wreath of evergreen; and set all around the wreath were lighted candles. A wreath of lighted candles! Their flames danced whenever Grandma moved. For a time Nancy could look at nothing but the wreath. She hardly heard when Grandma spoke to her.

"Oh, Grandma!" she said at last.

Then she realized that Grandma held a tray decorated with evergreen and lighted candles. On it were her silver coffeepot, cream and sugar, three cups, four saucers, and some Swedish coffee bread.

Every Lucia morning when Grandma was a little girl, her mother had come, dressed in white and with a lighted wreath on her head, to bring her the Lucia coffee. Every year, since Grandma was married, she had done the same thing for her family. Nancy knew that this morning, probably this very minute, Aunt Anna in her lighted wreath and white dress would be taking the Lucia coffee to Uncle John and the girls; and Aunt Martha with her lighted wreath would be going to Uncle Sven.

Grandma set the tray on the table near Nancy's bed, and she and Grandpa sat down so that they could all four have their Lucia coffee. (The fourth saucer was, of course, for Teddy.) The coffee bread was made in the shape of cats! Neither Grandpa nor Grandma knew the origin of this custom; they knew only that coffee-bread cats were the proper thing to have on Lucia Day!

Grandma kept her lighted wreath on her head; and they drank their coffee and ate their "cats" by the light from its candles and from those on the tray.

"The name Lucia means light," said Grandpa, "and Lucia Day is one more thing to remind us of the great Light of Christmas."

From this day on until Twelfth Night, he told Nancy, they must not let anyone who came to the house go out without first partaking of some hospitality. If they did, the Spirit of Christmas would go out, too. Everyone who came must be offered a cup of coffee, or a cooky, or one of the *karameller*, or something else to eat. It didn't matter whether they were guests or those who came to the house on errands as the milkman and the postman did.

When they had finished drinking their coffee, Grandma told Nancy to put on her bathrobe and

slippers. Grandpa wrapped her in a heavy blanket and carried her across the street so that she could be with Mrs. Brown and Alex and Ben when Grandma came in her lighted wreath to bring them their Lucia coffee.

From this time on Nancy was in charge of seeing that the Christmas Spirit did not go out of the Bensons' house. As soon as anyone came to the door, she was ready with a treat. Most of all, she liked to pass the *karameller*. But, of course, the people who came to the house often couldn't have one of these every time. Each could choose a *karamell* only once. Even so, Nancy had to keep on making more and more.

Now Grandma was busier than ever, baking and getting all sorts of things ready for Christmas.

On Saturday, Uncle Sven came for the children—all except Ben, who couldn't be spared from the grocery store—and they spent the whole day in Aunt Martha's kitchen, making Christmas wreaths and other decorations.

And then it was the last Sunday in Advent— the day when John August was to come.

But this Sunday was not a beautiful clear day, as the others had been. It had begun to storm in the night and by morning the storm was almost a blizzard. Grandpa went to church but he would not let Grandma and Nancy go out. When he came home again, he was worn out from fighting the wind.

"John was in church," he said, "but not Anna and the girls. And, of course, Sven and Martha did not get there. I'm afraid there'll be nobody but ourselves at the Advent candle lighting today. Certainly they won't dare take John August out. I don't even dare to try to carry Alex across the street in all this wind and snow."

It was a great disappointment.

"Whatever will Helga do?" asked Nancy. "She's been talking about this Sunday all month."

They felt sorriest of all for Helga.

"Her mother will have a hard time trying to comfort her," said Grandma.

But there was nothing they could do about it.

It was still snowing and blowing when it was time for the Advent candle lighting at four o'clock, but it was warm and cozy in the house. Oscar came in and lay down in the sitting room and Teddy sat in Grandma's lap.

"So there are five of us," said Nancy.

Grandpa and Grandma talked about Christmases they remembered from their own childhood, and from the time when their children were small. Nancy told about the happy Christmas days she had had with Mamma and Papa.

Then Grandma showed her an unusual thing.

"When I was a little girl in Sweden," she said, "I used to think the cats and kittens didn't get so much for Christmas as the other animals did. The horses and cows would get extra grain and hay, and we always saved some bones for the dogs. And the birds had their treat, too, but we couldn't spare more than the tiniest bit of milk for the cats. They were my special pets and I wanted them to have something very nice. So, long before Christmas, I used to begin to make them presents. I used to knit a pair of mittens for the front feet and a pair of stockings for the hind feet of every cat on the farm."

Grandma put her hand in the pocket of her dress and pulled out a small box. In the box was a little striped stocking that had once belonged to a cat in Sweden—many, many years ago.

The foot of the stocking was black; the leg had stripes going round and round—brown, orange, and black. The stocking was beautifully knitted, and Grandma had been only a little girl when she made it!

Nancy was completely charmed by the thought

of cats and kittens wearing mittens and stockings. She touched the little striped stocking gently.

"Where are the others you knitted?" she asked.

Grandma laughed. "I guess the cats lost them soon after Christmas," she said. "I don't suppose they thought so highly of their Christmas gifts as I did."

While Grandma and Nancy were talking about the little striped stocking, Grandpa said he would feed the animals and bring supper in to his two ladies, too. He set a little table in front of Grandma and put a tablecloth on it. Then he brought in bread and butter, meat and cheese, a pot of coffee and a pitcher of milk. They ate their supper with only the Advent candle for a light.

"We don't know what to give Ben for Christmas," Nancy said. "All he seems to want is to go back to the city."

"I know," said Grandpa, "and it is the one thing he can't do."

"Of course I want to be with Mamma and Papa," said Nancy. "But, oh, dear, I don't want to go back to the city. I wish Mamma and Papa could be here and we could all be together forever. But even if Ben's grandmother came here, I guess he'd still be lonesome for the city."

"Perhaps he would," said Grandpa. "He seems

to be happy here at times, and I'm sure the Taylors are good to him; but he's still lonesome underneath it all."

"Grandpa," said Nancy, "I know it costs an awful lot to travel. But do you think if we each gave a little money to Ben—not just the children but the grownups, too—we could get enough for him to put a dollar or so in the bank? And we could tell him that it was the beginning of a trip to the city, and maybe by summer he could have earned enough to go with it so that he could go to visit his grandmother?"

Grandma and Grandpa thought about Nancy's suggestion for a while.

"I think it might be a good idea," said Grandma. "It would give Ben something to work toward."

"I think so, too," said Grandpa. "I think it might help him. Let me talk to the Taylors about it first. Their friend would probably know some place where Ben could stay in the city for a week or two, so that he would have to pay only his fare. We could find out how much that would be and then Ben would know how near he was getting to his goal. It would be a great thing for him to have something like that to look forward to."

"You were a thoughtful girl to plan that, Nancy," said Grandma.

Now Nancy read the Christmas story:

" 'And there were in the same country, shepherds abiding in the field, keeping watch over
their flocks by night. . . .' "

Teddy purred loudly in Grandma's lap; Oscar
thumped his tail now and then, and the candle
flame grew brighter, and then suddenly went out.

Now it was Christmas week. On Friday it
would be Christmas Eve.

*Chapter 10*

It was the whitest, most beautiful Christmas week any of the children could remember. Grandpa said it was one of the most beautiful ones he could recall. He had to put away Karl the Twelfth's grocery wagon and take out his sleigh instead. Karl the Twelfth's sleigh bells jingled merrily every time he started out or came back home again. It would have been a good time for sliding, but that would have to wait until after Christmas. The children had no time for it now.

Usually they had two weeks' vacation at Christmas, but this year they had only one. Now and at

Easter they would have to make up for the time they had lost because of the fire in their school.

"And just when we need the time at home most," said Sigrid.

Still, they all agreed that they wouldn't have given up the topsy-turvy weeks.

Grandma cleaned her Advent candleholder and put four new candles in it.

"We will burn them all at once on Christmas Eve," she said.

"And have candles in the windows, too, and on the tree," said Nancy.

"Of course," said Grandma.

Nancy still had not finished all her Christmas presents; and she and Alex had to keep making more and more *karameller*.

The Taylors liked Nancy's plan for Ben, and the children collected two dollars for him. Nancy made him a calendar so that he could cross off each day as it went by.

Packages kept coming—from Papa and Aunt Marion; from Uncle George and Aunt Hanna. Nancy had a Christmas letter from her mother. It was a long, long letter. Mamma had been writing it a little at a time when she felt strong enough.

It told about the friends Mamma had made in the hospital, especially the children, and what they were doing for Christmas. It told about one lady who had been in the hospital when Mamma first got there, but was now well again. Because she knew how much Mamma loved flowers, this lady sent her a little plant or a cut flower or two each week. Mamma thought she could save some of the plants to take home so that Nancy, too, could see them someday. The letter even told about what Mamma had to eat and who her nurses were and what they said and did. It told how much Mamma was looking forward to being with Nancy again.

"That is a lovely letter," said Grandma. "You will want to save it always."

"It is almost like a little book," said Nancy.

"After Christmas you can make it into a book," said Grandma. "There is still some of your yellow rose wallpaper left. You can paste it onto cardboard and make covers for the letter."

"A little yellow rose book!" Nancy said. "I will save it always."

She and Grandma decorated the house with Christmas greens and candles. Uncle Sven brought in the Christmas tree, and one evening Alex and the Carlson girls came to help trim it. They were having Christmas trees of their own, of course, but they wanted to help with Grandma's, too.

Alex and his mother were going to his grandmother's for Christmas Eve and Christmas Day. Grandma worried about Ben—it was hard for a child to be unhappy at Christmastime—and she was relieved when Nancy told her what he had said.

"I asked him what he was going to do on Christmas Eve," Nancy said, "and he told me that he and Mr. Taylor were going to be very busy as soon as he got home from work on Christmas Eve, and on Christmas Day and Sunday, too. I asked him what they were going to do, and he said he couldn't tell yet."

"Did he look sad about it?" asked Grandma.

"No, *glad*," said Nancy. "I think it must be a Christmas surprise, but I don't know why it would take Sunday, too. And Alex told me that he and his mother are coming home Sunday morning; and he doesn't know why, because they usually stay several days at his grandmother's. He asked his mother if they were coming for some special reason and she said yes. But she wouldn't say what the reason was. Alex said something must be going on that we don't know about."

"Well, Christmas is the time for secrets and surprises," said Grandma, "and we mustn't ask questions."

And then it was the morning of Christmas Eve. Of all the days of Christmas, this was the one that meant most to the Swedish people—this, and the early morning service in church on Christmas Day.

Nancy was up early, but Grandma was up long before her. When Nancy came downstairs, Grandma had already put her big iron kettle on the stove to cook the beef and pork which would make the rich broth for "Dipping Day."

Even before she had had her breakfast, Nancy had to go into the sitting room to look at the Christmas tree. It was so tall it touched the ceiling.

It was beautiful in the daytime with its tinsel and glittering balls and snowy white popcorn strung in long chains. It would be even lovelier at night, lighted by the small wax candles fastened to the branches. Then the star at the top would glow in the flickering light.

Grandma had already spread her Christmas cloth on the dining room table. It had been woven by hand and embroidered in Sweden. The cloth was white, and all around its border were *tomte gubbar*—the little Swedish Christmas elves—and poinsettias and Christmas bells. This tablecloth had been part of Grandma's Christmas for many years. The Carlson girls loved it and would have felt that Christmas was not complete without it.

In the center of the table was a bowl of holly. Mrs. Brown had given Grandma this, and she was very proud of it. She had never had real holly on her table before. Mrs. Brown must have bought it in a florist shop. The table was all ready for the Christmas Eve supper.

They were going to have their noon meal in the kitchen in spite of the fact that there would be many guests in the house. After she had had breakfast, Nancy helped Grandma get ready for it.

They did not set the table in the usual way. Instead, they placed a tall pile of plates, another of saucers, and a group of cups at one end of the table. Near these Nancy put the shining silver knives and forks and spoons.

"Not everyone will eat at once today," said Grandma. "Not everybody has the same time off from work at noon, and people will have to come when they can, to 'dip in the kettle.'"

Grandpa had told Nancy about this Christmas Eve meal. He said that once upon a time there was a great famine in Sweden. People had nothing to eat but thin broth and black bread. Still, they celebrated Christmas. They dipped their bread in the kettle of broth, sang their Christmas songs, and made a feast of their famine. In memory of that time, and the bravery of those courageous people, other Swedish people followed the custom of "dipping in the kettle" at noon on Christmas Eve.

But now the broth was rich and good; and the bread Grandma made for Christmas was the best Nancy had ever tasted. She did not think she would care much about the broth, but she changed her mind the minute Grandma let her taste a little piece of dipped bread. "It's wonderful!" she said; and she was not surprised that people came from near and far to dip in Grandma's kettle.

A little before noon, Grandma put some sausage into the broth to cook—this took only a little while, not nearly so long as it did to cook the beef and pork.

At noon Grandma sliced large platters full of beef and pork and sausage. She put plates of Christmas bread on the table, too. Her largest coffeepot was on the stove ready with the first supply of coffee. "We'll have to make more," she said.

Soon after twelve o'clock, Grandpa came. He had Mr. Taylor and Ben with him. Next, Uncle

Sven and Aunt Martha arrived. Then neighbors began to come in—Mrs. Hackett who owned the yellow rosebush Nancy loved so much; Mrs. Lindstrom whose parrot rode on the carpet sweeper and called, "Hurry up! Hurry up!" whenever she swept her floors; and Grandpa Kramer who told Nancy and Alex such good stories. All wanted to taste the "dipping kettle" meal and to share in the Christmas festivity.

Uncle John, Aunt Anna, Mr. Sanborn, and the three girls arrived; and more and more people kept coming.

They dipped their bread and ate it; and drank their coffee; and talked and laughed. Every once in a while somebody would begin to sing one of the lovely old Swedish Christmas songs, and all who could would join in.

Nancy did not wonder that Swedish people loved "Dipping Day."

By three o'clock most of the "dippers" had gone; and Aunt Anna said the children must all lie down and take a long nap.

"I'm sorry to have you miss any part of Christmas Eve," she said, "but you know you will be up until midnight and then have to get up almost as soon as you go to bed."

Nancy hated to go to bed now. The Carlson

girls didn't want to go either; but they remembered from other years how wonderful the Christmas Eve festivities and the early morning service in church were, and they wouldn't have missed either of them. It was worth taking a nap now in order to be allowed to stay up later.

Aunt Anna made the going to bed easy. She said, "I know that Mrs. Brown has left a book for each of you under the Christmas tree. If you like, you may open those packages and take the books to bed with you."

The children were delighted.

"Let's open one at a time," said Sigrid, "to make the opening last longer."

They sat down under the Christmas tree, and Grandma and Aunt Anna sat down on chairs close by to rest for a few minutes and to watch the children.

Sigrid's book was *Little Women*. Helga's had poems and stories in it, and colored pictures. She was sure she could read some of it herself, but, first, when she got upstairs, she would look at every picture. It seemed that Mrs. Brown knew how to choose books for little girls of all ages.

Nothing could have pleased Nancy more than the one she found in her package. It was *Mary's*

*183*

*Meadow*. Now she could read over and over again the story of Traveler's Joy. When she went home, she could take the book with her, so that Mamma, who loved flowers so much, could enjoy it, too.

Elsa's book was a thick one with many pages. None of the children had heard of it before, but Grandma and Aunt Anna were much interested to see that it had been translated from the Swedish, and that it was by a great Swedish writer, Selma Lagerlöf. It was called *The Wonderful Adventures of Nils*. Elsa wanted to begin it at once.

"Let's go up to bed, *quick!*" she said.

They went downstairs about six o'clock, refreshed and rested after their reading and naps. Grandma gave them each a bowl of bread and milk, and then Aunt Anna took them upstairs to get ready for the evening.

Nancy thought the Swedish Christmas Eve supper was as unusual as the noon meal had been. For one thing, it was to be served at half-past ten!

"This day is as upside-down as the topsy-turvy weeks," she said.

The girls had decided that they would like to wear either a red or a green dress because these were the Christmas colors. Luckily they each had one.

Sigrid and Nancy wore the school dresses Aunt Martha had given them early in the fall. Sigrid's was green plaid gingham, and Nancy's red plaid. Of course Elsa and Helga had received plaid dresses, too, but they were rose and blue. However, they had jumper dresses that were the right colors. Elsa's was green, and Helga's red. They wore these with white blouses.

Now Aunt Anna said they might open one more present. She knew what it was and she thought they should have it at once. She handed Sigrid a package.

Sigrid read what was written on it: "To Four Good Friends. From Whoa Emma, Danny, Cicily-Ann Sinkspout, and Cuckoo Clock."

When they opened the package, Elsa said, "These animals are just as good as Mrs. Brown at choosing the right thing at the right time!"

In the package were hair ribbons about an inch wide. Green ribbons for the two girls dressed in red. Red ones for the girls in green.

When the children came downstairs again, Grandma said they might each have a sprig of holly.

"Real Christmas children, such as you have been this year," she said, "should wear a little holly in their hair."

The green leaves and red berries of the holly matched all the dresses.

"You do look like Christmas children, every one of you," said Aunt Anna.

Grandpa and Uncle John came from work about seven o'clock; and Uncle Sven and Aunt Martha came about eight. Now everybody was there except the special company. Helga was the only one who did not know who this was to be. She did not even know that there was to be any special company. They had not dared to tell her for fear she would be too much disappointed if things did not go as they had planned.

When, a little after eight, the doorbell rang, Sigrid, Elsa, and Nancy pretended they were hurrying to the door, but they let Helga get there first. Uncle Sven told her afterward that Santa Claus must have heard her screech of surprise and delight clear up at the North Pole.

There on the doorstep was John August in his father's arms, and standing near him were his mother, his uncle, and his aunt. Grandma had decided to invite them for Christmas Eve because they could not come on the fourth Sunday in Advent.

"Besides," she had said, "it will be so good to have a baby in the house again on Christmas Eve."

And that was what everybody kept saying over and over again that night.

John August wore the christening dress his mother had made for him and embroidered with the most delicate embroidery.

"It is like the christening robe the King's son wears in the fairy tales," said Elsa.

"I thought I'd let him wear it because it's Christmas," said his mother.

The children agreed that it was right for him to be dressed in his best because of the important part he would have to play that night.

"It's up to you, young fellow," Grandpa told him, "to lead the Long Dance of Christmas Eve."

The youngest person in the house must lead this dance; the oldest come last, with all the others, going up by ages, in between. Everyone must hold hands with the person in front of him and the one in back of him. Helga had expected to lead the dance, but she was delighted to give her place to John August. His father carried him. Grandpa put some red cord on Mr. Nelson as if it were reins. Helga held these with one hand and took Elsa's hand with her other one.

The procession went into the front hall and up the stairs. Into one room and then into another John August and his father led them, with everybody skipping along behind. Only Aunt Anna stayed down in the sitting room to play Christmas music on the piano.

"Wait until we get downstairs again," Elsa whispered to Nancy. "Just wait! It's *beautiful*."

Now John August led them down the back stairs, into the kitchen, through the dining room, and to the door of the sitting room. The gas lights had all been turned off, but every candle on the tree was lighted and the star shone at the top.

They gathered in front of the glittering tree and sang the Christmas Eve song. This was one that Nancy, too, could sing in Swedish.

> Happy Christmas Eve! So clear and shining,
> Now the candles are lighted in our hearts
> and our homes. . . .

After the song, John August's mother laid him in the clothes basket which Grandma had made into a little bed for him. It stood near the Christmas tree. John August fell asleep almost instantly and slept peacefully through all the laughing and talking, the singing, and the opening of Christmas presents. He did not wake up when, at half-past ten, everyone else went into the dining room for the Christmas Eve supper.

Like the Dipping meal at noon, the Christmas

Eve supper was always the same year after year. Its main course was a kind of fish called *lutfisk*. The children didn't like it, but the grownups considered it a great delicacy.

"I don't blame you, girls," Aunt Martha said. "I didn't like it when I was your age, but now I wouldn't change it at Christmas for anything else in the world. You'll feel the same way someday."

The children did like the rich butter gravy, though, and the potatoes and Swedish Christmas bread. And they liked the Christmas rice pudding served for dessert with sugar and cinnamon and cream.

Most of all, they loved the excitement of being up so late, the Christmas tree, the shining candles, and the songs.

This Christmas Eve meal was always planned so that it would be over just before the clock struck twelve.

About five minutes before midnight, Grandpa stood up and all the others stood with him. John August's father went to the clothes basket and picked up the sleeping baby, who woke up at once and looked as good-natured as when he had fallen asleep.

His father looked a little guilty.

"Perhaps I shouldn't have picked him up," he

said, "but I did want him to be awake when his first Christmas comes."

The children thought he had done exactly right. Of course, John August should be there with them all when Christmas came.

Now Uncle John opened the front door wide, and as soon as they heard the church bells strike twelve, they began to sing the Swedish Christmas psalm they all loved: "All Hail to Thee, O Blessed Morning!"

Nancy knew that they had done this every year since they could remember. It was, Grandpa had told her, the best-loved moment of all their Christmas season.

*Chapter* 11

ALTHOUGH they had stayed up until John August and his family went home a little after midnight on Christmas Eve, even the children were to be allowed to go to the early morning service in church on Christmas Day. Aunt Anna woke them at half-past four.

"Wake up, chickens!" she said. "Wake up! It's Christmas Day."

Aunt Martha came upstairs, too, to help the girls get dressed quickly. They had all been sleeping in Nancy's room—two in the bed, and two on a mattress placed on the floor. Their stockings hung in a row at the foot of the bed.

"Santa Claus has been here!" said Helga, jumping up and down. But there was no time to look at presents now. Even stockings would have to wait until after church.

Downstairs, the candles were lighted in all the windows and even on the Christmas tree. The grownups were having coffee and rolls, standing around the kitchen table as they ate. The children took their rolls and the cups of cocoa Grandma had ready for them, and ate their early breakfast sitting under the lighted tree.

"This is a most unusual place to have breakfast," said Elsa.

Uncle Sven and Grandpa were already harnessing Whoa Emma and Karl the Twelfth to their sleighs. Soon everyone was ready.

They rode through the dark, frosty morning, with sleighbells jingling all the way. Many houses had lighted candles in the windows, and some had lighted Christmas trees. Grandpa said it was because not only the Swedish people in town but others, too, loved the Christmas morning service, and got up early to go to the Swedish church.

"It's not at all the way it was when we went to see the sunrise in September," said Nancy. "Then hardly anybody was up. Now almost everybody seems to be. Sleighbells are jingling everywhere."

When they came to the church, many people were going in through the wide-open doors. Nancy could hear the organ playing.

She took hold of Grandma's hand and walked beside her out of the darkness into a church ablaze with lighted candles in every window and on the altar. At the front of the church stood two tall Christmas trees—much bigger than those in Grandma's sitting room—with hundreds of little wax candles glowing among their branches. The lovely fragrance of evergreen branches filled the church.

Nancy sat between Grandma and Elsa and listened to the music and watched the candle flames flicker and dance on the Christmas trees.

There were more people in church than there were on Sunday or at any time except at this early Christmas morning service. Every pew was full, and extra chairs had been brought in. Still there was not room enough for all. Many people were standing at the back of the church.

The organ began to play the Christmas psalm the Bensons and their guests had sung at midnight. Everybody in the church stood up. It was wonder-ful to sing "All Hail to Thee, O Blessed Morning!" with the organ, and with all the other people in the church singing, too.

After the song was over, the minister read from the Bible. He began, " 'The people that walked in the darkness have seen a great light. . . .' "

"Everything for Christmas seems to be about light," Nancy thought. Grandpa had even told her that it was on Christmas Eve that the days began to lengthen and grow lighter. She sat back and looked at the tall white candles on the altar and tried to count the little flaming candles on the trees.

After a while Helga fell asleep and her father picked her up and held her in his lap; but Sigrid, Nancy, and Elsa stayed wide awake.

When the service was over and they came out of the church, it was daylight, and people were calling to each other:

*"God Jul! God Jul!"*

*"Merry Christmas! Merry Christmas!"*

The children spent the rest of the morning looking at their presents, playing their new games, and reading the books Mrs. Brown had given them.

At noon they all had Christmas dinner at the Carlsons' house. Nancy's dolls, Charlotte and Jasmine, were invited, too. Uncle John had brought home a little Christmas tree not more than fifteen inches high. It stood beside the big tree in the sitting room. Sigrid and Elsa had made tiny decorations for the little tree as a surprise for Helga; and all their dolls sat around it.

"I've never seen a doll's Christmas tree before," said Nancy. "Hereafter, I'm going to trim one every year myself."

After dinner the girls had to take naps again so that they would be wide awake for the early evening service in the church.

This service was the children's own festival. They sang their songs and spoke their pieces, standing in front of the great lighted Christmas trees. There was a present under the trees for every child in the church.

The festival made the end of the day as lovely as the beginning.

Grandma told Nancy that the day after Christmas was also a holiday in Sweden. It was called *Annandag Jul.*

"That means Second Christmas Day," she said.

Nancy thought this was a very good idea. "It's kind of like an 'afterparty,' I guess," she said.

"So it is," answered Grandma.

This year the day after Christmas was a holiday

in America, too, because it was Sunday. Grandpa and Uncle John did not have to go to work and could be with their families all day.

Nancy slept until noon. She was astonished when she came downstairs to find that it was not breakfast time but time for Sunday dinner instead!

"Well, I ought to be rested now," she said.

"You look fresh as a daisy," said Grandpa. "How would you like to go sleigh riding this afternoon?"

"Sleigh riding!" said Nancy. "Oh, goody! Are the Carlson girls going, too? And Alex?"

"We're all going," said Grandpa, "grownups and children."

"Right after dinner?"

"No," said Grandpa. "Alex and his mother have just got home and they need a little time to rest. Between three and four they'll be ready."

"Are we going to the farm?" asked Nancy.

"No," said Grandpa, "I thought we'd ride out and have a look at the little house."

Nancy was so excited at this news that she forgot to ask how Karl the Twelfth could carry them all. She soon found out that he wouldn't have to.

Uncle Sven and Aunt Martha came. They were not riding in their Sunday sleigh but in one that was very much like Grandpa's grocery sleigh. There would be plenty of room for everybody.

They set out just before four o'clock. It was such good sleighing weather that Whoa Emma and Karl the Twelfth did not even know that they were pulling such big loads. The sleighs slid over the hard-packed snow as if there were nobody in them.

As soon as they got out into the country, Uncle John began to sing, and they all sang with him:

Jingle bells, jingle bells, jingle all the way,
Oh, what fun it is to ride in a one-horse open sleigh!

and

Deck the halls with boughs of holly,
Fa, la, la, la, la, la, la, la, la.
'Tis the season to be jolly,
Fa, la, la, la, la, la, la, la, la.

and all the gayest, merriest carols they could think of.

They sang one funny Swedish one. It didn't seem to make much sense but they loved it anyway:

Now it is Christmas again,
Christmas again,
Christmas again.
Now it is Christmas again,
And Christmas will last until Easter.

"I wish it would," said Helga.

But even the Swedish Christmas wasn't so long as that.

Of course Whoa Emma got to the road of the little house first, but Uncle Sven made her wait for Karl the Twelfth and his sleigh full of people so that they could all go up to the house together.

Not one of the children had guessed that a surprise was waiting for them. Sigrid was the first to get an idea of it.

"There's a light!" she almost screamed. "There's a light in the little house!"

"There are candles in the windows!" said Elsa.

"There's a *Christmas tree!*" said Nancy.

Mr. and Mrs. Taylor and Ben stood on the doorstep, waiting to welcome them. The grown-ups had never seen Ben look so happy.

The children noticed only the little house.

Mr. Taylor had taken the boards off the sitting room windows. There was no furniture in the room except a few chairs, and some cushions and blankets on the floor. But there were candles in all three of the sitting room windows. Standing in front of the boarded-up fireplace was a great Christmas tree, decorated with popcorn and cranberries, shining apples, and a silver star at the top.

"The tree was Ben's idea," said Mr. Taylor. "I helped him cut it down and bring it in here, of course, but otherwise he has done all the work on it himself. He made the decorations and trimmed the tree."

The children forgot all about asking Ben whether he liked his present or not; they were so thrilled with what he had done for them.

"And you kept it a secret from all of us!" said Grandpa. "Good for you, Ben."

Now Mr. Taylor brought in another surprise— the picture. He set it up beside the Christmas tree, and the golden-brown colors in it glowed in the light from the Christmas candles.

The grownups all thought the little girl was an unusually lovely child, and Sigrid and Helga were as sure as Nancy and Elsa were that she must be Mariette.

"*Of course* she is," said Sigrid.

Even Alex had to admit that the little girl looked as if her name were Mariette.

"But how does it happen that we could have Christmas in the little house today?" asked Sigrid. "What will the Cranes say?"

"The house doesn't belong to the Cranes any more," said Grandpa.

"Doesn't belong to the Cranes!" said Elsa. "But

it has to. They couldn't sell it out of the family."

Grandpa repeated what he had said. It was true that the little silver house didn't belong to the Cranes any more.

"But whose is it?" asked Alex.

"How could they sell it?" asked Nancy.

The children asked questions so fast that they gave Grandpa no chance to answer them.

"If you'll all sit down on the floor," he said, "and not interrupt too much, I'll tell you the whole story.

"You remember how much interested Uncle George was in this little house. He has always liked it, and, after we came out here on the moonlight ride, he liked it more than ever. It seemed to him it would be a perfect place for Aunt Hanna and him to live after he retired from his work. After Mr. Maple told you that a law firm had charge of it, Uncle George found out what firm it was and went to see the lawyers."

"Was what Mr. Maple said true?" asked Elsa.

"Yes," said Grandpa. "Old Jacob, as you always call him, left the property tied up so that it had to be kept in the family. But Mr. Maple neglected to tell you one thing—because he didn't know it himself, I suppose. Old Jacob's will said that when the Crane family had died out—when there was no member of the family left—then the little house could be sold."

"And have they all died?" asked Sigrid.

"Yes," said Grandpa, "and here is something you children will say is as good as a fairy tale. The very week Uncle George went to see the lawyers, they were planning to put the house up for sale. If Uncle George and Aunt Hanna hadn't come to see us that week, and if we hadn't taken that moonlight ride, somebody else might have bought the little house."

"Oh," said Elsa, "wasn't it *lucky* they came? When are they going to move here? Right away?"

"No," said Grandpa. "Uncle George isn't going to retire for another ten years or so. He has rented the house to a family that will move in in the spring."

"Is it a nice family?" asked Nancy. "Will they love the little house?"

Grandpa smiled.

"Yes," he said, "it's a very nice family."

"What's their name?" asked Elsa.

Grandpa looked around at all the children sitting at his feet, and then he answered Elsa's question.

"Their name is Bruce," he said. "Mr. and Mrs. Bruce, and Miss Nancy Bruce."

"NANCY!" said Alex and the Carlson girls.

Nancy turned so pale that Aunt Martha put an arm around her.

"I thought for a minute you were going to faint," she said.

"It was Aunt Martha's idea that you might move into the little house," said Grandpa. "Tell them, Martha, how you happened to think of it."

"It came to me," said Aunt Martha, "the day Nancy and Elsa and I went out to the little house and found the yellow rosebush, and felt so sad that Nancy would not be here to see it blossom. I knew living in the country would be good for her mother; and I knew that Uncle George had already begun to think of buying the little house. We don't need to tell you the whole story tonight. It all took a great deal of letter writing and arranging, of course, but at last it is settled. Nancy's father has been able to get a job in the shoestore in town; and as soon as her mother gets out of the hospital she will come to Grandma's or to the farm. And in May the little house will be ready for you, Nancy."

"Oh, Nancy!" said Elsa, "you'll be with us forever and ever. You won't have to leave us at all."

"Nancy!" said Sigrid. "Won't we have fun! I'm glad Old Jacob was ornery and kept the house boarded up until you came!"

"That's another thing," said Grandpa. "Elsa was evidently right about Old Jacob. He wasn't so bad as the rest of you thought. He made a great deal of money and left it all to be used for a children's ward in a hospital. The money Uncle George is paying for the house will go to the hospital, too."

"Old Jacob must have done it in memory of his little daughter, Mariette," said Elsa.

"You may be right," said Grandpa. "Perhaps we'll find out someday."

"We'll find out everything," said Alex, "about the house and the picture, too. Maybe we'll even find treasure."

"We can plant seeds for Traveler's Joy," said Elsa.

"We can make things and have a sale and give the money to the children in Old Jacob's hospital," said Sigrid.

"And, Ben," said Helga suddenly, "when you've saved up enough money to go to the city, you save up enough to come back, too! So we can all be together forever and ever."

Grandpa put his arm across Ben's shoulders.

"That's right, Ben," he said. "We can't get along without either you or Nancy."

Nancy had not said anything at all. The surprise had been so great that she was just beginning to realize that she and Mamma and Papa were really going to live in the little house, and she wouldn't have to leave her friends. She got up and went over to Grandma.

"It's almost too much to believe all at once, isn't it, darling?" Grandma asked, hugging her.

Nancy nodded. She stood close to Grandma listening to the other children talking eagerly about things the Crimson Ramblers could do to help get the little house ready, until Grandpa said it was time to go home.

But Mrs. Taylor said they must all come over and have a cup of coffee or cocoa first.

"It's no trouble at all," she added. "It's practically ready."

They found that the Taylors had a little parlor organ and that Mrs. Taylor could play on it. And that Mr. Taylor liked to sing as well as they did themselves.

Instead of leaving early, as they had intended to, they stayed so long singing with the Taylors that the stars were out and the moon was shining when they set out for home.

Nancy stood up as they rode by the little house. The moon shone down on its gray boards just as it had done the night they first saw it.

She put her hand on Grandma's arm.

"See, Grandma," she said. "It *is* a little silver house."

JENNIE D. LINDQUIST was born in Manchester, New Hampshire, and attended the University of New Hampshire and the School of Library Science at Simmons College in Boston. She has been concerned with books for young people most of her life. Until very recently she was the editor of *The Horn Book*, a magazine devoted entirely to children's books.

Before that, Miss Lindquist was the children's librarian in Manchester, Consultant in Work with Children and Young People at the University of New Hampshire Library, and head of the Children's Department for the Albany Public Library. During the summers she taught a course, "Appreciation of Children's Books," at the University of New Hampshire.

THE GOLDEN NAME DAY and THE LITTLE SILVER HOUSE are her only books for children. Of them the author writes: "They are not autobiographical, but are drawn from recollections of my own childhood. My grandparents came to America from Sweden when their children were little, and —like the children in the books—I was brought up on two sets of holidays and festival days, the Swedish and the American."

GARTH WILLIAMS was born in New York City of parents who were both artists. Educated in England, he graduated from the Royal College of Art in London, and won the British Prix de Rome for sculpture in 1936. He later spent considerable time in many of the large capitals of Europe. During World War II Mr. Williams was in London, serving with the British Red Cross.

Mr. Williams and his wife and two daughters now live in Aspen, Colorado, where he devotes most of his time to illustrating and writing children's books.

He has illustrated THE GOLDEN NAME DAY by Jennie D. Lindquist, THE TALL BOOK OF MAKE BELIEVE, the "Little House" books by Laura Ingalls Wilder, E. B. White's CHARLOTTE'S WEB and STUART LITTLE, Margaret Wise Brown's THREE LITTLE ANIMALS and LITTLE FUR FAMILY, THE HAPPY ORPHELINE by Natalie Savage Carlson, and many, many others. In addition, Mr. Williams is the author-artist of two books, THE RABBITS' WEDDING and THE ADVENTURES OF BENJAMIN PINK.